W9-BRF-818

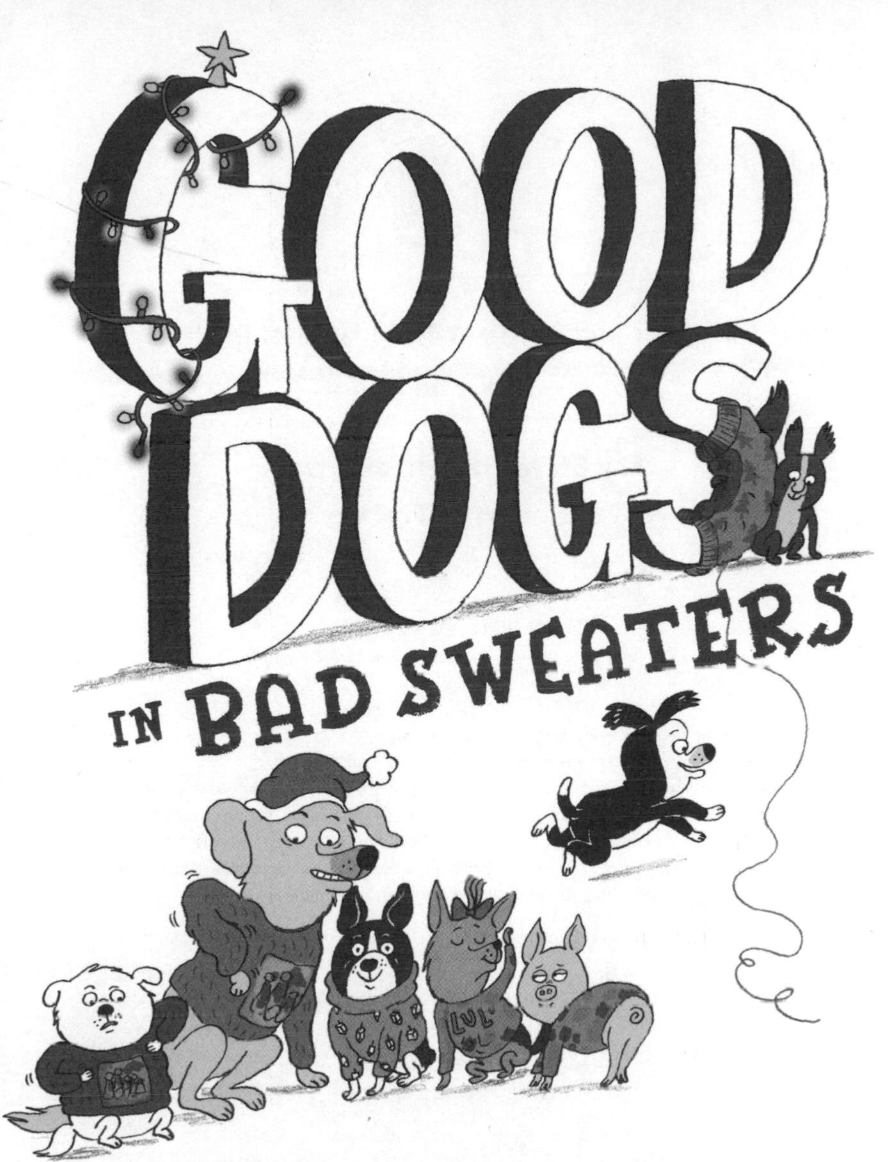

Rachel Wenitsky + David Sidorov

illustrated by Tor Freeman

putnam

G. P. PUTNAM'S SONS

To our parents, for making us dog people

—R.W. and D.S.

For Steve, Steven, and Bob

Love from Tor xx

G. P. PUTNAM'S SONS

An imprint of Penguin Random House LLC, New York

Visit us online at penguinrandomhouse.com

Library of Congress Cataloging-in-Publication Data is available.

Printed in the United States of America

ISBN 9780593108505

1 3 5 7 9 10 8 6 4 2

SKY

Design by Eileen Savage and Suki Boynton

Text set in Chaparral Pro, Archer, and Johnston ITC Pro

Hurry up and fetch all of the Good Dogs adventures!

Good Dogs on a Bad Day

Good Dogs with Bad Haircuts

Good Dogs in Bad Sweaters

CHAPTER 1

"GO ON, BUDDY, fetch!" Erin shouted as she threw the tennis ball across the dog run, which had been spruced up with twinkly lights draped over the wire fence.

King leapt into the chilly air, excited. "It's happening again!" he yelped, running after the ball for the fifteenth time that chilly afternoon. "She threw it again!"

The very good dogs of Good Dogs doggy day care hadn't been coming to the park all that often now that it was December and getting cold, so they were trying to make the most of it.

Hugo shook his head as he sat in the shade and watched his friend. "That's how fetch works, bud," he barked back.

"I know! I know! But I still get so surprised!"

"Come on, Waffles," Hugo said, nudging his floofy little sister with his nose. She was still a lot smaller than him but getting bigger (and floofier) every day. "Why don't you go play with King?"

"In a little bit!" Waffles replied. "Lulu is teaching me how to find my best angle. Can I get an Instagram so I can become a celebrity like her?"

"Maybe. But come on," Hugo pleaded. "You're so good at fetch! Lulu, did she tell you she set a new fetch record in the backyard with Zoe the other day?"

"*You* told me," Lulu said. "Twice this morning."

"Right. Well, did I tell you she got an award at

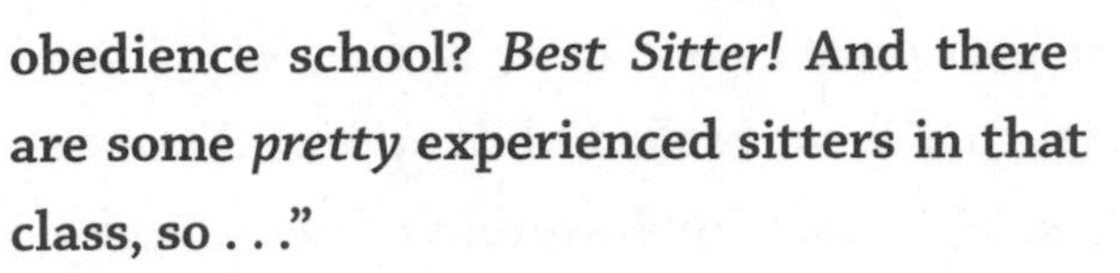

obedience school? *Best Sitter!* And there are some *pretty* experienced sitters in that class, so . . ."

Waffles whined. Hugo knew he was embarrassing her, but he just couldn't help himself. He was a proud big brother!

"An award?" Lulu's ears perked up. "I *love* awards. Last year I won an Instagrammy for Best Dog Dressed Like a Cat . . . Dressed Like a Dog. It's on the shelf next to my bed, and I chew on it every morning."

"I guess it *was* pretty cool to win an award," said Waffles, tossing her head back. Lulu's approval seemed to mean a lot to Waffles. "But I wouldn't know *anything* about sitting if it weren't for Hugo. I'd probably be standing my whole life!"

Hugo beamed. He and Waffles had bonded a lot over the past few months since she'd become part of his family. He looked across the park, where King was zooming around in circles with the ball in his mouth. King's big sister, Cleo, a German shepherd mix, and Petunia, the playful one-year-old pit bull, ran over to join him. The wise old sheepdog, Patches, was slowly walking laps around the edge of the dog run and muttering happily to himself, his usual routine.

"What should I do now?" Hugo heard King bark.

"Give the ball back to Erin . . . ?" Cleo suggested. "So she can throw it again?"

"Oh yeah! Of course!" King said, and he ran over and dropped the ball at Erin's feet. "Fetch, Erin! Fetch!"

"*You* don't have to say it to *her*," Cleo explained.

Hugo laughed. "Should we join them?" he asked Lulu and Waffles.

"I think I'm good," Lulu said. "We're about to start filming my new reality series, *Hot Dog!* And my hair *finally* grew back to normal. So I really can't afford to take a ball to my moneymaker right now."

Hugo gave her a puzzled look.

"Sorry, *moneymaker* is what we dogs in the biz call a 'face,'" Lulu explained. "And *biz* is what we in the biz call the 'Bizarre Job of Entertainment.' I think."

Hugo and Waffles both nodded. Lulu had been talking about her new show nonstop. It wasn't going to be on the big rectangle in the living room, she had explained, but it *was* going to be on a pet-themed "streaming app" called Waggo. Hugo couldn't keep track of the rapidly changing media landscape, but it mostly didn't matter, because he was a dog. And it was true, Hugo noticed. Lulu did look a lot more like Lulu than she had with the strange haircut she had had the previous month.

"I can't believe you're going to be a movie star," said Waffles, staring at Lulu in awe.

"Well, not yet," Lulu said with a sigh. "But the web series was a big hit, so this show is just going to be about *me*. It could be my big break! If I do a good job. Which I will, obviously!"

Lulu sounded very confident, but her tail flagged just a teeny bit. It was a small thing, but Hugo could tell she was nervous.

"Of course you will, Lulu," Napoleon said reassuringly as he sauntered over and sat down next to Hugo. "You've got this. I believe in you. We all do. All you need to do is keep believing in yourself."

Napoleon had recently started training to be a therapy dog, and Hugo still hadn't gotten used to the French bulldog's new positive personality. He even wore a new harness that said "Comfort Dog in Training." Lately, it felt like Napoleon loved supporting his friends and talking about their feelings as much as he loved eating sandwiches and digging holes. Not to mention, he had quietly become one of the best-behaved dogs in town. As part of his training, he was going into hospitals and nursing homes to help sick people feel better.

Hugo was surprised that Napoleon had gone into this line of work, but it seemed to suit him perfectly. Just like being his own family's assistant, schedule keeper, shoe finder, dog treat taster, couch sleeper, and Waffles's big brother suited Hugo. Hugo was inspired and impressed that his friend was making the world a better place.

Cleo and King came running over to Hugo, Lulu, Napoleon, and Waffles.

"Did you see that?" asked King, excited as ever. "I ran after the ball like a hundred times! And Erin said I was a good boy! Did you hear Erin say I was a good boy? Jin thinks I'm a good boy too! He said so this morning. Did you hear Jin say I was a good boy?! Well, first he asked me who was a good boy, but then he answered his own question and said it was ME, and actually he says it every morning and—"

"Calm down, King," Cleo said, and she demonstrated taking a deep breath in and out. "I noticed! Jin loves us! Who wouldn't? We're adorable."

Ever since Erin and her longtime boyfriend, Jin, had gotten married, Hugo had watched King and Cleo welcome Jin into their family with outstretched paws. Jin even helped Erin out at Good Dogs some days, and the good dogs loved him very much.

Just then Hugo heard a noise from above and saw Nuts the squirrel dart out of the leaves of a nearby tree.

"Dog!" Nuts squealed, running back and forth on a branch. "Dog here! Dog there! What? How? Why? When?"

Nuts was famously a very nervous squirrel, and Hugo had seen him bug out before, but this was really something. The good dogs were regulars at this dog park, so why was Nuts surprised to see them?

"What's going on, Nuts?" Cleo asked, calm as ever.

"Well," he said, staring at them all intensely from above. "I just saw Waffles over by the skating rink. But *here is Waffles* right below me, again! Does Waffles have super-squirrel speed? Is Waffles in two places at once?! Something suspicious is going on! Something spooky! Something scary! Something totally weird! WHAT. IS. HAPPENING?"

Nuts stood over their heads, panting, his tail twitching, with a wild look in his eyes. They all stared back until Lulu finally broke the silence.

"Nuts are you, like . . . *okay*?" she asked.

Nuts sighed, then scurried down to join them on the ground. "I haven't been sleeping," he explained. "Berries is going to have our babies any day now!"

"Oh my dog! Babies!" Hugo said. "That's so exciting! Congratulations."

"Mazel tov!" Napoleon added. "That should be cause for celebration."

"I was a baby once," Patches recounted, with a far-off stare. "I enjoyed it very much, as I recall. You see, the year was 1967, I'm pretty sure, the summer of love, and—"

Hugo didn't think there was any way Patches could be that old, but Nuts interrupted before he could say anything.

"You don't get it!" he shouted. "Squirrels can have up to *seven* babies at one time! Do you have any idea how many mouths we'd have to feed? That would be . . ."

Nuts counted on his tiny squirrel fingers. "SEVEN!" he shrieked. "And we still have so much to do! Build a nest! Stock up on acorns! I don't know if you guys have noticed this, but I never know where my acorns are!"

The dogs all nodded. They had noticed.

"What kind of dad can't even find his own acorns?" Nuts continued. "Don't get me wrong—I am *so* excited to be a dad and meet my babies. But I'm gonna have to *really* step up while Berries is recovering. And WINTER IS COMING! THAT'S ONE OF THE COLDEST SEASONS, I THINK. AM I SCREAMING? I FEEL LIKE I'M SCREAMING!"

"Wow, there's a lot to unpack there," Napoleon said thoughtfully, taking a couple of steps toward the twitching squirrel. "It sounds like you love Berries very much and you want to be helpful!"

"I do! I love her so much!" Nuts said, nodding.

"Well, she loves you too. And you're going to work as a team and figure this all out together. You know what they say: 'Family is everything.' At least that's what the pillow my mom put on the sofa says."

"You're right," said Nuts, calming down a bit. "You're so right. Thanks, Napoleon."

Nuts started breathing normally again. And just in the nick of time too, since Erin was now standing near the fence with their leashes.

"King! Cleo! Hugo! Lulu! Waffles! Patches! Petunia! Napoleon!" Erin called out. "Come here, everyone!"

"Good luck, Nuts," Napoleon said. "You're gonna be great!"

And with that, they all ran off to form a perfect line in front of Erin. She leashed them up, and they made their way through the park and back toward Good Dogs doggy day care, which was also Erin's house.

"The holidays will be here before we know it! What's everyone doing this year?" Hugo asked.

"Jasmine and I are going to celebrate Christmas at home," Lulu said. "We usually go to Minnesota to see her fam, but my show is shooting a special Christmas-themed ep. Sorry, *ep* is what we in the biz call an 'episode.' Anyways, I think she's a little sad about it, but I'm sure we'll have an awesome Christmas, just the two of us."

"What about you, Napoleon?" Hugo asked. "Any Christmas plans?"

"We celebrate Hanukkah," Napoleon said proudly. "Which means that I'll be getting *eight* presents. One for each night. We already started!"

All the dogs oohed and aahed. Eight presents! That sounded pretty great.

"Eight presents is nothing," King exclaimed. "Erin celebrates Christmas *and* Hanukkah, which means we'll get whatever eight plus one prezzies is! What is that, Cleo, like a million prezzies or something?"

"That's nine, King," Cleo answered. "And you forgot to mention the latkes . . ."

Napoleon nearly started slobbering all over the side-walk, and King's tail wiggled back and forth joyously.

Hugo was about to ask what a latke was when King suddenly started growling. There was a man dressed as Santa Claus at the entrance to the park collecting money for charity. King must have been confused and upset by the man's big red coat and beard. He started tugging on his leash while Petunia let out a few anxious barks, and even Cleo and Patches seemed a bit uneasy. The man was ringing a bell, and Hugo had to admit the bell made him a little nervous too. Why did bells have to be so loud?

Erin pulled King back and steadied the dogs. "It's okay, guys," she said soothingly. "It's just Santa."

"Yeah," Waffles chimed in as Erin pulled them all away from the man. "Santa's the best! He brings presents to boys and girls all over the world. He lives in the North Pole and rides a cool sleigh and has the best beard! I love Santa! We have no reason to be afraid of him!"

Petunia looked unsure. "Did a human tell you that?" she asked. "Sounds like typical human nonsense to me. Even if that does happen, we dogs are *totally* left out of the fun. As usual!"

"No way!" Waffles said, jumping up and down. "Santa has a *dog*! His name is Santadoodle, and he leaves presents for all the dogs in every family! He puts treats and toys *in their owners' shoes*! Can you imagine finding a present inside the most delicious-smelling thing in the house? I can't wait!"

Hugo scowled and cocked his head to the side, surprised to hear this. He'd lived through enough Christmases with his family to know that Petunia was right—Santa was mostly for the humans. Sometimes he'd get a nice chew toy, or a couple of treats, but he'd never gotten a special present in Enrique's shoes, or anyone else's. And he'd *definitely* never heard of

Santadoodle. Zoe must have told Waffles about Santa, Hugo figured, but he'd never heard any of the kids talk about Santa's dog.

"Santadoodle sounds pretty great, Waffles," Hugo said. "Who told you about him?"

"My mom!" Waffles answered. "When we were strays, before we all got taken to different shelters, she told me and my brothers and sisters all about Santadoodle and how someday we'd all live in loving homes where Santadoodle would come and give us presents! She used to get gifts from Santadoodle when she had a human family, I guess. I can't *wait* for my first visit from Santadoodle. I'm going to stay up all night on Christmas so I can see him!"

Hugo didn't know how to respond. He locked eyes with Lulu, who gave him a look as if to say, *Don't worry about it.* But Hugo was already worried.

He wondered if Waffles's mom had made up Santadoodle to make her puppies feel better. Or maybe her original owner celebrated Christmas with Santadoodle and presents in shoes. Hugo knew different families had different traditions. But he didn't want to burst Waffles's bubble. He imagined Waffles waking up on Christmas morning and looking in Zoe's shoes only to find them empty. She would be crushed. Devastated. Her Christmas would be ruined!

If Waffles wanted a visit from Santadoodle, Hugo decided, she was going to get a visit from Santadoodle. But how?

He wished more than ever that his humans could understand his barks and whines and pants. Then he'd be able to walk right up to them and say, "Mom, Dad. Waffles is expecting a gift for Christmas inside someone's shoe! I know it sounds strange, but you have to trust me on this!"

But that would be impossible. So that meant it was up to Hugo to make Santadoodle happen.

LATER THAT AFTERNOON, back at home, Hugo dug around in the front hall closet. Mom had left it open, and Hugo was trying to find something, *anything*, that he could leave for Waffles on Christmas.

Maybe she'd like an extension cord? He sniffed at it a bit. *No, probably not. What about this basket full of yarn?*

He chewed on a ball of yarn for a moment, trying to imagine finding it inside a shoe.

Nah, too itchy.

Then he smelled something interesting in the back of the closet. He pawed a bunch of junk out of the way to reveal an old Frisbee! Perfect! This would be just the thing.

Ol' Hugo, he thought to himself, *you're too good at this. You've already got it all figured out!* He re-buried the

Frisbee for later and trotted out into the living room, where Waffles was on the floor on her back, watching cartoons with Zoe.

"You know what *I* want from Santadoodle?" Hugo said, testing the waters. "A nice old Frisbee. Maybe a striped one that's been chewed a little. Doesn't that sound great? Do you know about Frisbees, Waffles? They're hard and they fly through the air and sometimes they whack you in the face if you don't catch them just right, but it doesn't really hurt."

Waffles rolled over and blinked at him. "Um, yeah, Hugo. I have, like, three Frisbees in the yard," she answered. "You can borrow one, if you're so hot for Frisbees. I think they're okay, but kinda boring. It's like somebody flattened a ball by accident. I bet Santadoodle will get us something cooler than that."

Hugo lay down and put his face in his paws. *Oh boy. This is going to be harder than I thought.*

CHAPTER 2

LULU AND JASMINE were sitting on the couch, wearing matching fuzzy slippers and fluffy pink bathrobes. *It's so adorable when humans wear dog clothes,* Lulu thought.

"I'm so sorry," Jasmine was saying into her rectangle. "But we just got the filming schedule, and it goes right into the holidays."

Lulu wagged her tail at the people inside the rectangle, Jasmine's parents. Lulu loved them and always looked forward to seeing them, even though lately it had been mostly inside the rectangle.

"So . . . you can't come home for Christmas this year?" Jasmine's dad asked sadly.

"I wish we could," Jasmine said. "But airfare to Minnesota is too high after we're done filming. And we'd only get to be there for a day or two. It just won't work out."

"That's too bad," Jasmine's mom said. "Your brother won't be here, either. He's spending winter break with his new boyfriend's family. We're happy for him, but the holidays without you or Jack just won't be the same."

"Plus! We were really excited to introduce you *and* Lulu to the newest member of our family . . ." Jasmine's dad added.

"It's Buttercup!" Jasmine's mom shouted, and then she lifted into the rectangle someone—some*thing*—that Lulu had never seen before. It looked like a pig, but . . . it was the size of a small dog. Was it a dog pig? Or a pig dog?

"You got a teacup pig?" Jasmine laughed. "You guys must be getting pretty lonely without me and Jack at home, huh?"

"No way!" Jasmine's dad said. "We have each other! And now we have Buttercup too. We adopted her from a rescue! Anyway, guess you'll just have to wait to meet her another time."

"What is this series anyway, honey?" Jasmine's mom asked. "Who films over the holidays?"

"I told you! Lulu's going to have her own show!" Jasmine reminded them. "On this new streaming app, Waggo. It's all short episodes—they're calling it 'chewable' content—designed to be watched in chunks while you're waiting for your dog to do its business, or something like that. The schedule's tight because they need a lot of shows ready when they launch. It's a pretty big deal. They're even rebooting that show *Prank'd* with Lil' Stinky."

"Will it be on TV? You'll have to tell us when it's on TV."

"No, it'll only be on phones," Jasmine explained. "But if you turn it sideways—"

"Will you be acting in it too, honey?"

"Well, no," Jasmine said. "I'll be in it, because I'm her owner. But not really acting. It's real life! I've actually stopped auditioning for the time being to concentrate on it."

"Really?" Jasmine's dad asked as he scratched Buttercup under the chin. "But you love acting."

"It's fine," Jasmine said, and Lulu felt her hand stroking her fur. "Lulu's dream is my dream now. She could become a huge star! And I'm finding that I'm pretty good at managing Lulu's career . . . Maybe that's what I'm *supposed* to be doing."

"Okay, honey," Jasmine's mom said supportively. "Whatever you want. Just don't lose sight of what makes you happy."

When the rectangle conversation was over, Jasmine scooped Lulu up and took her to the closet to show off a brand-new outfit. "This is for the shoot tomorrow, girl!" she said excitedly as she opened the closet door. "Your Christmas look!"

Lulu's jaw dropped as she saw the "outfit" that was hanging in front of her: a sparkly, spiky, pointy doggy suit in the shape of a star. It made *quite* the statement, and Lulu was impressed by the effort that must have gone into making it. It looked like the type of star that might go on top of a Christmas tree, except it was big enough for a dog to fit inside. There were all sorts of lights and ornaments hanging off the thing, a small hole for her face, reindeer antlers for her head, and was that an *electrical cord* coming out of the sleeve? Jasmine set Lulu down and plugged the cord into the wall, and the whole costume lit up.

"They're going to put you on top of the tree!" Jasmine exclaimed. "It's going to look so cool!"

Lulu walked over to the outfit, rubbing her face against it—

OUCH! The star was made out of something scratchy. *Really* scratchy. It was like rubbing up against that one really spiky bush at the park. Lulu *loved* stars—she *was* one, after all—but she wasn't sure if she wanted to wear one. Especially one that felt like this. And she loved trees too—they were one of her favorite things to pee near and bark at—but did she really want to sit on top of one for several hours under bright lights?

"The producers loved your wild haircut at the wedding," Jasmine said, sensing Lulu's reaction. "They want you to push the envelope! You're creating new fashion trends for dogs."

Lulu remembered that her artsy, experimental look had been a big hit. Maybe this Christmas look would be too . . .

Okay, Lulu thought as she trotted into the bedroom to start her elaborate nighttime routine. *I'll give this a try.*

After all, maybe this outfit would be the thing that made her a huge star! Literally *and* figuratively! If the *Hot Dog!* series brought Lulu all the fame she'd ever dreamed of, then any uncomfortable outfit would be worth it.

DIRT! DIRT! GRASS! Dirt! OBSTACLE! JUMP, KING, JUMP! King's inner monologue raced as he dashed and darted around the agility course.

Dirt! Dirt! RAMP! OBSTACLE! Dirt! Dirt! Hurdle! Whoa—is that some pee over . . . King turned his head toward the source of that sweet, sweet smell, but then he snapped out of it.

No, King! Bad! he thought. Then, *Sorry, King! You're a good boy! That's okay, King! You're trying your best, King! Thanks, King!*

King was impressed with himself. He was almost through the agility course, and he had only stopped twice to smell pee, three times to chew on sticks, once to bark at a sound, and twice just for a break. He was improving, all thanks to his more relaxed attitude.

There are some things you can't control, buddy, he thought to himself as he ran through an inflatable tunnel, remembering some helpful advice Napoleon had given him. *You just gotta take it as it comes. If only the rest of the good dogs could see me now!*

He knew that while he, Erin, and Cleo were at the agility contest, Jin was running Good Dogs for the day. King's friends were probably all hanging out in the park with Jin. Except for Lulu, who must be at her big film shoot by now. King crossed the finish line triumphantly and jumped into Erin's arms.

"Good boy, buddy! You finished the whole course!"

They waited for a few other dogs to finish, then listened to the man in the green hat as he announced the winners on the Small Dog Course. King didn't expect to hear his name—finishing the course and making Erin happy was enough of a prize—but he listened just in case.

"Bronze medal goes to Lady Bird. Silver medal, Bowie. Gold medal, Rosie. And we have a few Honorable Mentions here . . . including . . . King! Congratulations. Also . . ."

The man handed Erin a small medal and then kept naming other dogs, but King didn't hear him because he was too busy barking with excitement.

Honorable Mention?! Wow! King had no idea what those words meant, but he assumed it was just another way to say *awesome dog* or *good boy.*

"That's amazing, buddy!" Erin said, scratching him under the chin. "I'm so proud of you! Now, come on, it's almost Cleo's turn."

They walked over to the Large Dog Agility Course, where Cleo was stretching and getting ready to run. King watched while Erin coached her and cheered her on.

"You've got this!" Erin shouted as Cleo bolted through the course. "You're fast! You're strong! Yep—jump, girl! You can do it!"

King couldn't see too well through the fence, but he was sure Cleo must have been doing perfectly, because she always did. But to his surprise, when Cleo crossed the finish line, she put her tail between her legs and looked straight at the ground, avoiding eye contact with Erin. King had never seen her look so disappointed, especially not after an agility contest.

"Hey, girl," Erin said, petting Cleo. "You did good! Two minutes, forty-one seconds . . . Good time! Not bad at all."

But Cleo kept looking at the ground.

"What's wrong?" King asked her.

"I knocked over an obstacle," Cleo said, and then she kicked at the dirt with her paw. "Ugh! It's a mandatory penalty!"

King also didn't know what *mandatory penalty* meant, but from the look on Cleo's face, he guessed it wasn't good.

"This is *not* okay," Cleo continued. "I'm a *professional*. Professionals don't make mistakes like that!"

King thought that must be true, because he'd never seen Cleo knock over an obstacle before. She was always the most athletic, agile, and technically perfect dog at these contests, and she usually won the gold or silver. But today, as the man in the green hat announced the winners, for the first time since King had known her, Cleo didn't win a medal at all.

Erin knelt down and rubbed Cleo all over, then held out a T-R-E-A-T in her hand. But Cleo looked away.

"Hey, it's okay," Erin whispered to Cleo. "Happens to the best of us. You still did great! And hey! You've got another chance to show off your skills in a couple of days at the holiday celebration . . ."

But Cleo just huffed and started walking slowly toward the car with her head hanging. King followed close behind his big sister. He wanted to do something to make her feel better.

"I wasn't in the zone. I wasn't focused," Cleo muttered to herself. "Wasn't on my A game. Didn't bring it. Maybe . . . I don't know. Maybe . . . I'm getting soft! I've been too distracted by all the changes at home."

When they got in the car, King snuggled up against Cleo and rested his nose on her back. "It's okay, big sis," he whined comfortingly. But she just looked out the window. King sighed. He had no clue what to do. Cleo was usually the one who comforted him when he was upset, or nervous, or sad, or hungry, or full of too much energy, or confused, or if he had to poop but needed to wait because they were in the car, or all of the above.

King had never seen Cleo like this. He knew he had to help her feel better. But how?

CHAPTER 3

HUGO SAT IN the back seat with Waffles and Sofia as the tall downtown buildings passed outside the window of the minivan. Enrique and Zoe were in the middle seats, with Mom and Dad up front.

"First Santa picture with Waffles!" Dad said, turning around while Mom parked the car. "Is everyone excited?"

Hugo wagged his tail to tell Dad that yes, he was *very* excited! Then he turned to Waffles and helped her adjust her sweater. Hugo knew that the matching Christmas sweaters were probably the most important part of this family tradition. Every year, the whole family wore green-and-red sweaters and went down to Pet City, the biggest pet store in the longest strip mall, to sit down with Santa and have their picture taken for their annual holiday card. And every year, their sweater had last year's picture on the front—so today they were wearing sweaters with pictures of themselves wearing sweaters with pictures of themselves wearing sweaters and so on. Hugo thought it was very clever, even if the sweater itself was a bit itchy and ill-fitting.

As they piled out of the car and into the store, Hugo stayed close by Waffles's side, thrilled to guide her through her very first family Christmas sweater photo. There was a *very* long line. So long that Hugo couldn't even see Santa up ahead, just an endless sea of legs.

"I thought we had a reservation," Sofia said, a little annoyed.

"We do—it's at seven fifteen," Mom replied, looking at her watch. "I don't know why there's such a long wait."

"I don't *like* lines!" Zoe stomped her foot. Hugo had a special talent for noticing when his family was stressed, and he could sense there was about to be a meltdown. So he nuzzled up into Zoe's side and let her pet his chin.

"Enrique! Where's your sweater?" Dad asked.

"It was hot! I took it off!"

"Where did you put it?" Mom asked. "Oh no. Don't tell me you lost your sweater."

Hugo's mind jumped into what he liked to call Solutions Mode. When there's a problem, nobody finds a solution better than Hugo! So he nuzzled up into *Mom's* side and let *her* pet his chin. This was usually his go-to when no other solution immediately presented itself.

Admittedly, if more than one person was stressed, that posed a problem, since Hugo unfortunately only had one chin.

"I found it!" Sofia said, retrieving Enrique's sweater from a nearby leash display. Crisis averted! But the tension still felt high . . .

"Hugo! Look! Look!" Waffles yelped from . . . somewhere. Hugo turned and saw that she wasn't by his side anymore. *Uh-oh! Did Waffles wander off somewhere?*

Hugo followed her voice down another aisle and around a corner, until he found his little sister standing with a handful of other dogs and their humans. They were watching a teenager in a Pet City uniform show off a bright, beautiful, blinking ball.

"Waffles, what are you—"

"Shh . . . Hugo, look," Waffles said, mesmerized.

"The Ultimate Ball is the pinnacle of doggy playtime," the teenager announced. "With thirteen LED lights, motion sensors, more than a hundred pet-friendly sounds, and an extra-thick chew-tastic rubber core, it's the perfect toy for any energetic pup! Watch this!"

She bounced the Ultimate Ball on the ground, and the whole thing flashed brilliantly like a rainbow. It made a delightful squeaking sound as it hit the floor, then a jingling tune, like music, as it flew back up into the teenager's hand.

Waffles couldn't take her eyes off the ball. "That's it," she said softly to Hugo. "That's what I'm going to ask Santadoodle for. *The Ultimate Ball.* She said it was chew-tastic . . ."

"And when you sync it up with the app, you can download . . ." The teenager kept talking, but Hugo didn't understand most of her big human words.

"Hugo! Waffles! There you are!" Mom's voice shouted from down the aisle. "You can't run off like that!"

"Let's go! Come on!" Dad yelled, patting his knee for the dogs to come. "We're about to miss our photo! It's our turn!"

Hugo and Waffles ran down the aisle and followed the rest of the family as they rushed to the back of the store, where Santa was sitting in front of some cameras and lights.

"Oh, there you are!" the photographer said. "We're behind schedule, so let's get you in there quick."

"My hair! Mom! I need to fix my hair," Sofia fretted. "Can I go to the bathroom?"

"We don't have time, honey," Mom replied. "Just sit down and smile, everyone!"

Dad bumped into Enrique as they scrambled toward the chairs. Hugo hadn't seen the whole family this anxious and frazzled since Enrique lost his backpack the previous month.

"Huh, that's weird," the photographer muttered to himself as the family finally got seated and turned toward the camera. "I just photographed another dog that looked *just like* that one. Do you have two families, pup?"

He was pointing to Waffles. Hugo thought that was odd, but he didn't have time to wonder about it, because it was time for the photo.

"Here we go!" Santa said. "Say 'cheese'!"

Waffles barked wildly. She loved the word *cheese* because she knew it meant the *food* cheese, and she must have thought that Santa had cheese for her.

"Enrique! Your sweater is—" Mom started.

Snap! And just like that, the picture was over.

"Inside out," she finished.

"Next in line!" the photographer barked as their picture printed. Hugo followed his family as they got up from their seats, and Dad grabbed the photograph. It was . . . interesting. Zoe was blinking, and Mom was in the middle of talking to Enrique, whose sweater was on totally wrong. Sofia looked upset. Dad was smiling but looking in the wrong direction. Hugo thought he actually looked pretty nice, and Waffles too! She was mid-bark, but it looked cool. Hugo was looking right at the camera, tongue out like a good boy. Like a very good boy.

"No time for redos," Dad groaned. "Guess this is our holiday card."

Everyone was still grumpy as they walked out of the store. Hugo tugged on Mom's shirt and tried to get her attention.

I need to show them the Ultimate Ball! he thought. He needed to let them know that Waffles wanted it for Christmas. It really would be the perfect gift. He let out his best pay-attention-to-me whine.

Moooooom, he tried to tell her. *Check out this toy that Waffles wants!* Mom always understood him when he was hungry or had to pee or needed her to rub his belly. Maybe, just maybe, she would understand him now. But she didn't.

"Not now, Hugo," Mom said, leading him out into the parking lot. "Let's go home."

As soon as Hugo stepped into the parking lot, he stopped in his tracks. There was Waffles, already on the side-walk, with her sweater off, wearing a leash held by a man Hugo had never seen before! *What's going on here?*

"Waffles?!" Hugo barked.

"What?" came a familiar bark from behind him. It was Waffles's voice. He turned around and saw Waffles *again*, still wearing her sweater, standing next to Dad. He turned back to Other Waffles, then back to Waffles again. Hugo hadn't been this confused since Enrique had found his backpack in the refrigerator. *Two Waffleses? How is this possible? And what's the plural of Waffles?* Hugo's mind raced with questions. *Is this what the photographer was talking about? A Waffles clone? But how?*

The man holding the leash also looked confused. He called out to Hugo's family.

"Hey there! Looks like we got dog clones or something!" the man said, pointing to Other Waffles and then to Waffles. Then Waffles and Other Waffles saw each other, and they both let out shrieks of pure delight.

"FUZZFACE!" Waffles barked. "Oh my dog, oh my dog! It's Fuzzface! Hugo! It's my littermate!"

Waffles ran over to Fuzzface. She couldn't stop wagging her tail. Hugo followed her over

to sniff this new dog hello. The humans chatted above them as Waffles and Fuzzface caught up and jumped all over each other.

"I haven't seen you in so long!" Fuzzface said, licking Waffles playfully.

"Your butt still smells the same!" Waffles barked, smelling Fuzzface's butt. "How have you been, Fuzzface?"

"Oh, that's not my name anymore," he explained. "Now I'm Bentley Furmuffin the Third. They call me Bentley for short."

"That's a great name!" Waffles said, and then she turned to Hugo. "Our mom used to call him Fuzzface! Because he has fuzz on his face."

"Oh! That makes sense," Hugo said. "What did she call you?"

"She called me Fuzzface too. Because I also have fuzz on my face. Sometimes she called me Floofo. Or Fluffbaby. Or Funkyhead. She was really good at names." Then she turned to Bentley, aka Fuzzface. "My name is Waffles now!"

"That's a wonderful name," Bentley replied. "I've heard that waffles are . . ."

"DELICIOUS!" Waffles and Bentley barked in unison.

"I've heard that too!" Waffles said. "I hope I get to try some soon!"

Up close, Hugo realized that Bentley and Waffles

really looked almost identical, except that Bentley had a small black spot on the tip of his left ear.

"After we got split up, we went to a really nice rescue in the next town over," Bentley told Waffles. "Me and our brothers and sisters and our mom. We were so worried about you! After a few weeks, we were all adopted. I was the last one to find my people, but once I did, they were so perfect! Oh, I ran into our mom once at the vet. She's doing really well!"

"That's so great to hear!" Waffles said. "My life is pretty amazing now too. This is my family."

Waffles nodded over her shoulder, where Enrique was pulling off his inside-out sweater and Zoe was begging Dad for a snack.

"They're the best," Waffles continued. "Zoe's my best friend, and Hugo is my dog best friend, and he's the one who brought me to Zoe and he teaches me everything and one time he even rescued me from a dumpster."

Hugo nodded, proud. It gave him a warm, fuzzy feeling to hear Waffles sound so happy about her life.

"I love my people too," Bentley said. Hugo looked up and saw that Bentley's parents were still talking to Hugo's parents. Bentley's parents looked a bit younger and didn't seem as tired.

"They give me *anything I want*," Bentley told Waffles.

"It's just me and them. I think they sort of treat me like I'm their human child, but better."

Bentley's mom knelt down to give Waffles a good pet. "This is so exciting!" she said, looking up at Hugo's family. "The rescue told us Bentley had siblings, but they'd all found homes by the time we got there. We would have adopted more if we could have!"

"She's adorable!" Bentley's human dad said. "Just like Bentley."

"She's a really special puppy," Dad responded. "And this is her big brother Hugo!"

Hugo felt a warm hand on his back as Bentley's dad introduced himself with a really nice pet.

"You should bring Waffles over sometime! For a playdate," Bentley's mom said. "And Hugo too, obviously!"

Waffles looked thrilled to hear this. Hugo gave a good hearty tail-wag because he agreed that that sounded like a lot of fun. After the humans exchanged information and said goodbye, Hugo turned over his shoulder and watched Bentley hop perfectly into his perfect car with his perfect people.

"My sweater was too itchy!" Enrique was whining. "That's why I had to take it off! Sorr—eeeee!"

Hugo didn't think Enrique sounded very sorry.

"Well, way to ruin the photo!" Sofia huffed back. "If you hadn't lost your sweater, maybe I would have had time to fix my hair!"

"I still want a snack!" Zoe whined.

"Kids, stop it," Mom called from the front seat. "We'll do better next year, all right?"

But as Hugo rested his head on Sofia's lap in the back seat, the kids continued to whisper-fight. Zoe shoved Sofia, whining that she didn't have enough space, and knocked Waffles off her lap. Hugo noted Waffles's sigh and the way she lifted her head to watch Bentley and his family disappear in their own car—probably filled with endless bacon treats and love.

He loved his family more than anything, but as he watched Waffles squirm back into Zoe's lap, he couldn't stop thinking, *Would she be happier with Bentley and his family?*

LULU COULDN'T *WAIT* to get out of her scratchy star outfit as Jasmine carried her home from the bus stop. They'd had a very long day on set—full of bright lights and lots of direction and some snacks and plenty of sitting around—and through it all, Lulu had had to wear the itchiest, pointiest, hottest outfit she'd ever worn.

Jasmine yawned a loud, long yawn as they got to their front door. "I can't wait to order a pizza and watch a bad Christmas movie, Lu," she said wearily.

And help me take off this star! Lulu thought. *That has to happen first!*

"Hmm . . . that's weird," Jasmine said as she put the key into the door and pushed it open. "It's open. Did I leave the door open this morn—"

"SURPRISE!!!"

Lulu jumped out of Jasmine's arms, startled, and landed feetfirst on the floor. She looked up to see Jasmine's parents! And they weren't even in the rectangle, they were in *real life—#IRL!*—standing in Jasmine and Lulu's living room with arms outstretched. And the room was different! There was a big Christmas tree, fully decorated, in the corner. And five stockings hanging on the wall. And a plate piled high with cookies sitting on the table. Lulu let the sweet, sweet smell fill her nose.

"Mom? Dad? Oh my—what are you doing here?!" Jasmine asked.

"We wanted to surprise you!" Jasmine's mom said.

"We know you keep the spare key under the plant outside, so we let ourselves in."

"We hope it's okay," Jasmine's dad said. "We did some baking this afternoon and set up some decorations. For the holidays!"

That's when Lulu smelled it—there was another pet in the house! She turned and saw Buttercup, the tiny pig she had met through the rectangle. Now Buttercup was in Lulu's kitchen, snuggled up in a fuzzy shark-shaped bed, under an equally fuzzy blanket. She looked cozier than the coziest pictures on #NationalCozyPetDay.

"Oh! We almost forgot!" Jasmine's mom said. "Jasmine, Lulu. Meet Buttercup!"

Lulu took some cautious steps over toward this tiny pig and gave her a sniff.

"Hey there!" Buttercup snorted. "You must be Lulu! Heard a lot about you!"

"Whoa," Lulu said, surprised. "You speak dog?"

"*You* speak *pig*?" Buttercup replied. "Anyway! You must be tired! I heard you were on set all day? What's a set? Sounds exhausting. I'm exhausted too, by the way. We drove here straight through the night. The traffic around Denver was pretty awful, but otherwise it wasn't so bad. Have you ever been to Cracker Barrel? My mom and dad got me this shark bed there this afternoon. It. Is. *Heavenly.* Apparently it's meant for dogs. There's room for two! Wanna join me? Oh, and *what are you wearing?* It looks so *itchy* and *pointy*! Take that thing off and climb into this comfy shark with your new friend Buttercup! Sorry I'm rambling. When I get tired, I get perkier and more alert and more awake, it doesn't make sense. Anyway . . ."

Lulu just stared. She wasn't sure what to make of the tiny cozy pig on her kitchen floor. But she knew Buttercup was right about two things: Taking off the costume *was* going to feel amazing. And that shark bed *did* look heavenly.

CHAPTER 4

KING LAID HIS head flat on the hallway floor, gazing into the laundry room, where Cleo sat by herself in the corner.

"What's up with Cleo?" Hugo whispered to him. Waffles and Napoleon walked over too, to see what was going on. It was just the five of them at Good Dogs today, with Lulu filming her series and Petunia and Patches home with their families, who were off work for the holidays. Normally King would have had a great time with this small crew—wrestling with Waffles, tugging on a stick with Hugo, wrestling *while* tugging on a stick with Cleo, having a long, emotionally honest conversation with Napoleon—but today he'd spent the whole morning watching Cleo, who had spent the whole morning pouting in the corner of the laundry room.

King had spent enough miserable time sitting in

the laundry room, the gloomiest room in the house, to know exactly how she felt: sad. The laundry room was where Erin and Jin put King when he was in trouble. But Cleo wasn't in trouble! She was just *choosing* to sit alone in the laundry room all day, with its strange-smelling carpet and baskets of weird underwear.

"She's upset about the agility competition yesterday," King told his friends. "She didn't do as well as she usually does. I wish I could help cheer her up."

"Aha." Napoleon nodded wisely. "That sounds difficult. I've seen this in my work. She clearly needs to get those feelings *out*. Allow me."

King watched Napoleon walk into the laundry room. He couldn't hear what Napoleon said to Cleo, but he could clearly see her response. She reached out with a paw and pushed him over, knocking him to the ground. Napoleon stood, shook it off, and stumbled back into the living room.

"I don't think she's ready to work through it yet," Napoleon told King, Hugo, and Waffles. "And that's okay."

"Well, then what can we do to make her feel better?" King asked, standing up and pacing around the living room. "There's got to be something we can do! We're four smart dogs. Let's put our heads together! Like for me, when I'm sad, cheese usually helps me feel happy again. Because it's cheese."

The other dogs all nodded and murmured in agreement.

"That's true," Hugo said. "Cheese *is* cheese."

"That's it!" Waffles yelped. "Let's get Cleo some cheese!"

King, Napoleon, and Hugo thought it over. Cheese. So simple. So delicious. Could it work? King noticed his tongue was hanging out and he was slobbering all over the floor at the mere thought of cheese.

"That could work!" he said. "Yeah. Yeah. I like this idea. Who's a good idea? Who's a very good idea? Cheese is a good idea. Cheese is a very good idea."

"It's the best idea we've got," Napoleon agreed. Hugo nodded.

"It's a perfect idea," King added enthusiastically. "If we got some cheese from the fridge, we could really cheer Cleo up. Plus, *we* could probably take some cheese too."

"I was thinking the same thing," Waffles said.

"Same here, if we're being honest," Hugo added.

"Would be a shame not to," Napoleon said. "Once the fridge is open and all."

"So how do we do it?" King asked, ducking behind the coffee table to talk to the other dogs in private. Obviously, he knew that Erin couldn't understand them, but it still felt safe to be as secretive about Operation Free the Cheese as possible.

Operation Free the Cheese, King thought. *That has a certain to ring to it. Ring? Like a doorbell? No! Don't distract yourself, King!*

"Well," Hugo said, thinking. "Step one needs to be a diversion. Waffles! You should distract Erin with your unbelievable cuteness."

"Sorry, what did you say?" Waffles asked. "I was distracted by my own unbelievable cuteness. Just kidding—I'm in. I have a lot of experience with that."

It was true. King knew that Waffles was quickly turning into an expert attention-grabber. The plan was developing nicely so far.

"Step two! Napoleon!" Hugo commanded. "Do you know how to open a refrigerator?"

"I could, if only I had a spatula . . . ," Napoleon replied.

"I'll get you a spatula!" King barked, then remembered to lower his voice to a slightly softer bark. "I'll jump up on the counter and drop a spatula for you."

"Great," Napoleon said. "Then I open the fridge and Hugo gets in there to open the cheese drawer. You can do that, right, Hugo?"

"Of course," Hugo answered proudly. "Drawers, cabinets, you name it, I can open it. All it takes is a long nose, some strong teeth, and a *lot* of practice. And friends, I've got all three. *And then some.*"

"Perfect!" King said. "Then we'll call Cleo over and go to town on our pile of cheese! That's an expression.

We won't actually go into town. I mean we'll eat the cheese together. She'll love it!"

King felt his tail wag for the first time all morning. All he had needed to do was to talk it over with some friends, and now they had a perfect plan to cheer Cleo up. And plus, he was about to eat cheese! What could go wrong?

"Let's do this," King said, nodding to Waffles, who took off toward the corner of the living room, where Erin was sitting at the desk. Waffles lay down on the floor by Erin's feet, her belly up, her paws wiggling in the air.

"Awww, cutie!" Erin said. "You want a belly rub, huh?"

Normally King would join Waffles for some belly rubs, but he was a dog on a mission. So he, Napoleon, and Hugo inched toward the kitchen. He glanced over his shoulder to see Erin kneeling on the floor, rubbing Waffles's floofy belly while Waffles excitedly squirmed on the floor. Then Waffles stood up on her back legs, leaned her front legs on Erin's shoulders, and licked Erin's face.

"Wow! What got into you, Waff?" Erin laughed. "You're a little bundle of energy!"

Then Waffles did the classic puppy distraction move: She ran around in tiny little circles as fast as she could.

Nice, King thought. *That's what I'd do too.*

But then—she stopped running.

"Uh-oh," Waffles said, looking down at the floor.

"Uh-oh," King said, looking down at the spot on the floor where Waffles was looking. There was a small pool of pee.

"Uh-oh," Erin said.

"I got a little too excited," Waffles whined, turning her head to the other dogs.

"It's okay!" Hugo said reassuringly. "She'll have to clean it up. More time for us to grab this cheese!"

Hugo was right. Normally, peeing inside the house was considered "bad," but this time it was for a good cause!

Who's a good cause? Who's a very good cause? King thought. *Helping Cleo is a very good cause!*

As Erin grabbed cleaning supplies from the closet, King, Napoleon, and Hugo finished making their way into the kitchen.

Okay, King! You can do this! Time to jump up on that counter and get the spatula!

King stood on his back legs and tried to jump onto the counter. He was nowhere close, landing back on the ground.

Whoops! Not high enough! Come on, King, use those agility skills.

He took a few steps back and took a running jump.

OUCH! He collided right into the cabinets and flew backward.

"Use the chair," Hugo suggested as he and Napoleon pushed a chair closer to the counter. King nodded, then leapt up onto the chair. *Halfway there!* From the chair, he climbed onto the counter easily, but *WHOOPS!* As he scrambled onto the surface, he felt his butt knock into the toaster, and it flew off the counter and into the trash.

"Oh no!" King barked. "The toaster! That's Erin's favorite toaster in the whole kitchen!"

"That's okay, buddy," Napoleon said. "We'll grab it after we get the cheese. You're doing great."

That felt nice to hear. This new Napoleon was so comforting!

"'Nothing's impossible when you try your best'!" Napoleon added. "That's from another one of my mom's pillows."

King shook off the toaster mishap and tried to focus on the mission. All of Erin and Jin's kitchen tools were sitting there, in a tall metal cup underneath the cabinets, next to the sink. But as he looked for the spatula, he realized a *major* flaw in the plan.

Oh no, King thought. *What's a spatula?*

He looked down to Hugo and Napoleon. "You guys . . . ," he started. "This might be a silly question, but can you remind me what a spatula looks like?"

"It's the one that looks sort of like a long, flat spoon," Hugo explained.

"Right!" King yelped, but then he got confused again. "And the spoon is . . . which one, again?"

King knew he needed to move fast, before Erin finished cleaning up the pee in the living room, so he guessed. "Is it this one?" King tossed a utensil onto the floor. Then he sent another one down. "Or this one? How about this one?"

"Nope, nope," Napoleon answered. "Not that one, either."

"You know what, this will probably be quicker," King said, getting a great idea. With one swift move, he pushed the entire container of utensils off the counter. There was a loud *CRASH* as they spilled onto the tile floor below and scattered across the kitchen.

"Here it is!" Napoleon grabbed the spatula in his mouth and quickly popped the refrigerator door open.

"What was that noise?!" King heard his sister's voice and then turned his head to see Cleo standing in the kitchen doorway. "What's going on in here? Why's everything on the floor? King, why are you on the counter?"

"Um . . ." King scrambled to come up with an excuse. "Because I'm . . . counting! No better place to do that than on a *counter*, huh? See, one, four, twenty, I dunno . . ."

Napoleon walked over to Cleo, trying to take her attention away from the mess on the floor and the scene unfolding at the refrigerator, where Hugo was sniffing all around.

"You seem tense, Cleo," Napoleon said soothingly. "Sometimes when I'm stressed, I like to focus on my breathing. A deep breath in . . ."

"What's Hugo doing?" Cleo asked.

Hugo's head was deep in the fridge now. It looked like he was having trouble finding the cheese drawer. As Cleo took a step forward to get a better look, Hugo panicked and yanked on *something* as hard as he could.

A sliding plastic drawer flew out of the refrigerator and smashed into the wall on the opposite side of the room, sending eggplants, cabbage, and peppers rolling across the floor. A bag of beets thunked down hard enough to ooze red juice onto the linoleum. King wasn't sure what some of the food was, but he was *pretty* sure it wasn't cheese.

"Whoops," Hugo said, looking down. "I think that was the vegetable crisper. Not the cheese drawer."

Then Erin ran into the kitchen, hearing the commotion. "What on *earth*, you guys?"

A LITTLE WHILE later, King sat in the laundry room with Waffles, Hugo, Napoleon, and Cleo. They all had their heads buried in their paws, except for Cleo, who looked more confused than anything else. On the other side of the doggy gate, Erin had her hands on her hips.

"And you're all going to stay in there!" she said. "Until I can get this mess cleaned up." Erin shook her head, looking disappointed, then headed into the kitchen.

"What were you *thinking*?" Cleo barked to King as soon as they were all alone. "What's gotten into you? Don't you know better than that? And where's the toaster? I have so many questions."

"I'm sorry," King said softly. "It was called Operation Free the Cheese."

"It was?" Waffles asked.

"Yeah, in my head at least," King answered. He turned back to Cleo. "We were trying to get some cheese out of the refrigerator. For you. I thought it might help you feel better about losing the competition yesterday."

As soon as King said the word *losing,* he wished he hadn't.

Cleo's whole body got stiff, and she turned her head away, glaring into the wall. "Losing *one* agility contest isn't the end of the world, King," she said quietly, but from the tone of her voice King wasn't sure she really believed it. "You should know that better than anyone! And besides, I don't need anyone's help getting cheese. When I want cheese, I get it the right way: by doing a trick so perfectly and flawlessly that it can't be described in words and it makes Erin cry a little. If you'll excuse me, I think I have something in my eye . . ."

And with that, Cleo walked to the corner of the room and sat down, facing away from everyone. She stared out the window, whimpering softly. King turned back to his friends.

"So, that backfired pretty badly," he said. "We made a mess, got in trouble, and I somehow made Cleo feel even *worse.*"

"It's okay, bud," Napoleon said, rubbing his head into King's side. "We made a bad decision with the cheese. But don't worry too much about Cleo. Every dog works out their own issues in their own time."

King sighed. "I just . . . I wish I could cheer her up

somehow," he said. "She's my sister, and I love her! It hurts to see her this upset, especially right before the holidays."

"Actually, it's perfect timing!" Waffles barked. "Santadoodle is coming soon! Santadoodle will fix everything!"

King looked over at Hugo, who seemed worried. King had only spent one other Hanukkah-Christmas combo with Erin, and he'd never heard of Santadoodle. But Waffles seemed certain, and her eyes lit up as she went on and on about this dog from the North Pole.

"When Cleo wakes up and sees her biggest wish in the whole world inside Erin's shoes, she'll forget all about the agility contest! Maybe there's a Hanukkah-doodle too! And she'll get even more shoe presents!"

King wasn't sure what to think. He'd been a tiny puppy last holiday season. He remembered Erin giving him and Cleo some really great gifts and treats. He remembered Erin lighting some candles. He remembered the tree inside the house, and he would never forget eating latkes for as long as he lived. But he didn't remember any gifts inside a shoe, and Erin had never mentioned Santadoodle.

Plus, as he looked at Cleo in the corner of the laundry room, he couldn't help but wonder . . .

Even if she gets the best toys and T-R-E-A-T-S in the world, what if it isn't enough to make her happy?

CHAPTER 5

"ALMOST THERE!" HUGO'S mom said as she turned the minivan onto a street full of fancy new townhouses.

The whole family let out a "whoa," and Hugo and Waffles looked out the windows to see what all the fuss was about.

"Whoa" was right! Every house was decorated for Christmas, but not with just any kind of decorations. They were decked out top to bottom with the biggest and most beautiful displays Hugo had ever seen. One house had a whole herd of reindeer on the front lawn, with lights that made them look like they were about to take off for the skies. Another had a giant sleigh on the roof with a big inflatable Santa who waved his hand back and forth.

The street ended in a circle, so that once you reached the end, you had no choice but to turn around and go back the way you came.

There can't possibly be anything fancier than a street

that leads to nowhere, thought Hugo. *It's like having a dog bowl that's just for decoration.*

"I think this is the one," Hugo's mom said, pointing to the house with the most decorations on the block. They pulled into a driveway, and Hugo saw that Bentley's front yard had a shining Christmas tree, a snowman, and a giant dog bone, all made out of bright, twinkling lights.

"Wow," Waffles gasped. "If I were Santadoodle, this would be my first stop!"

Mom took Hugo and Waffles out of the car and rang the doorbell. The door immediately swung open, and Bentley's mom and dad were standing there with big smiles on their faces.

"Waffles! Hugo! Come in, come in!" Bentley's mom said. Bentley's dad was holding a tray of the most delicious-looking, tasty-smelling homemade dog treats Hugo had ever seen and smelled, and Bentley stood behind him, panting eagerly. The treats were so fancy, they would have put everything at the Chic Patisserie to shame!

"Whoa," Waffles said. "Hugo, get a load of those T-R-E-A-T-S."

"Those look so good, even I would eat them!" Mom said. Bentley's parents laughed.

Humans sometimes said stuff like that, and it always confused Hugo. Why *wouldn't* they want to eat treats? They tasted so good! Did they not like dehydrated chicken liver or something?

Then Bentley's mom bent down to pet Waffles. "Look at you, Waffles. Such a cutie. You really do look *just* like your brother."

"We're just running some errands," Mom said, giving Hugo a good pet with one hand and Waffles, then Bentley, a good pet with the other. "We'll swing by and pick them up in a bit. Waffles, Hugo, have fun and be good, okay?"

Then Mom was gone, and Bentley's parents led Hugo and Waffles into a giant living room with floor-to-ceiling windows and a magnificent crystal chandelier. The whole middle of the floor was taken up by a poofy heart-shaped dog bed.

"Waffles! Hugo!" Bentley excitedly ran back and forth, clearly wishing he could run in two directions at once. "I'm so glad you're here! This is my house. This is my bed. That's my mom. That's my dad. That's a couch. That's the rug."

He zoomed around the room, making Hugo dizzy.

"Settle down, Bent," Bentley's dad said gently. "Let's show your friends what we got them!"

Bentley's mom brought in two brand-new squeaky dog toys: one shaped like a bone for Hugo, and one shaped like a waffle for Waffles.

Wow, these people went all out, Hugo thought. *Where did they find a toy that looks like a waffle?*

Anyway, Waffles loved it. And Hugo found that his new squishy bone had just the perfect squeak. Soon, the humans settled on the couch, and all three dogs lay down on the rug, digging into their toys next to the cozy fireplace. Hugo felt totally relaxed.

"Fuzzface, it's so good to see you again!" Waffles cried, getting up to lick Bentley's face. Bentley eagerly licked hers back, then batted her playfully to the ground. Soon they were half wrestling, half snuggling, and both wagging their whole butts, tails flying. Hugo was pleased to see Waffles getting along so well with Bentley. They were just like brother and sister!

Oh, right, Hugo remembered. *That's because they* are *brother and sister!*

"Awww, aren't they all so precious together?" Bentley's mom said, leaning over to pat Hugo's head. "I wish we could keep all three of you!"

Hugo could have sworn he saw Waffles and Bentley exchange an excited glance, like they were hoping she *would* keep all three of them? But maybe he was imagining things. Maybe they were just excited to see each other.

"Let's put on our doggy playlist," Bentley's dad said, turning on the stereo. Music blared out of speakers that were hung around the room. It was a song that Hugo knew every word to by heart: "Who Let the Dogs Out."

A classic, thought Hugo. *This couple's got great taste!*

"Let's go get their snack," Bentley's mom said to his dad, and they got up.

As soon as they left the room, Bentley hopped onto

an ottoman and looked down at Waffles. "Are you so, so, so excited for Santadoodle to come?!" he asked, his tail still wiggling wildly.

"So, so, *so* excited!" shouted Waffles. "I can't *wait* to see what Santadoodle brings me. I bet it's gonna be something really amazing. I bet it's gonna be the new Ultimate Ball!"

"I wonder what I'm going to get!" Bentley said. "Maybe a ball, or a giant bag of treats, or a special bed! Or all of those things! And more!"

Waffles jumped all around the room, getting more and more excited. "Ooh, I wonder what I'll get! I hope Santadoodle knows what I want!"

"Well, Waffles, you have to *tell* Santadoodle what you want. Remember how?"

"Oh yeah . . . ," Waffles started.

"By howling your wishes up a chimney!" Bentley and Waffles barked at the exact same time.

Really? Hugo wondered. *This Santadoodle thing has so many rules!*

"To the chimney!" Bentley yelped.

"Now wait a second," Hugo tried to say, but the puppies had already bolted toward the fireplace and were howling up into the chimney. It was too late for Hugo to quiet them down.

"I want toys!" Bentley howled. "And a pillow shaped like a hamburger that's full of peanut butter!"

"I want a really fluffy bed!" Waffles howled. "And the Ultimate Ball! That's what I want the most!"

"I want treats!" Bentley added.

"Yes, lots and lots of treats! Awoooo!!!"

"Treats!"

"Treats!"

"Shh!" Hugo shushed. He knew different families had their own rules, but he was pretty sure no human enjoyed loud howling, even when it was aimed up a chimney. He tried to get between the two puppies to break up their little ball of noise and energy. But they were too busy howling.

"Treats! Treats! Treats! Treats!" Bentley and Waffles chanted, barking loudly into the fireplace. Suddenly Bentley's parents came running into the room.

"What in the world?" his dad asked.

"Bentley! Waffles!" his mom commanded with a kind voice. "Sit. Bentley, sit. Quiet!"

"Waffles, sit, girl!" his dad said.

Both dogs sat.

"Good dogs! Here you go," Bentley's mom said, and she handed them both treats from a new tray filled with even more homemade treats. Bentley and Waffles both looked at each other, stunned.

"It worked! Thank you, Santadoodle!" they shouted.

Bentley's dad laughed at the puppies' silliness, then gave Hugo one of the treats. Up close, it looked as incredible as it smelled, and it tasted even better than it looked. *Is that almond butter?* As soon as she finished her treat, Waffles started running around in circles.

"See, Hugo? We howled for treats," Waffles said. "And treats came! Santadoodle is real, and he's all around us!"

Hugo shook his head. These puppies were too much for him. He had to admit he was getting a little worn out. "I need a drink," said Hugo. "Bentley, where's your water bowl?"

"Kitchen!" Bentley said with his mouth full. "Down the hall to the right."

Hugo made his way down the hallway, stopping to look at the family photos that lined the walls. In every photo, Bentley's parents *and* Bentley were smiling and looking straight at the camera. Impressive. In one photo they were all smiling on a beach. In another they were all smiling in a beach house. In another they were all smiling on a boat headed toward a beach.

Wow, Hugo thought, *this family really likes the beach.*

He was about to reach the kitchen when he passed by a closet door that was slightly open. An incredible smell was wafting out from inside. Like . . . chicken? Or jerky? Or dog biscuits?

No harm in taking a peek, he thought. His own closets were always filled with fun secrets, like hidden tennis balls and delicious old shoes. He nudged the door open the rest of the way with his nose. Then his mouth fell open in shock.

The closet didn't have a *single* person thing inside. It was entirely dedicated to Bentley! The incredible smell was coming from a bag of Chicken Jerky Dog Biscuits, which just happened to be Hugo's favorite. There were several bags of those, and even more treats, plus a crate full of chewy ropes and stuffed animals, and a shelf covered in pristine, unopened toys! It was an entire closet dedicated to Bentley and anything a dog could ever want.

Then Hugo spotted it. Up on the highest shelf, there was a familiar-looking box: the Ultimate Ball! With all of its high-tech lights and buttons and thingamabobs. *Why would they have all these unopened toys?* Hugo wondered.

Then it came to him. *Christmas is right around the corner. These must be Bentley's Christmas presents.* He felt a little guilty about snooping, but this was by far the most incredible collection of dog gifts he'd ever seen. There was no doubt it was better than whatever he and Waffles were going to get. He hung his head as he shut the door and walked to the kitchen.

He remembered the funny look Waffles and Bentley had exchanged when Bentley's mom had said she'd like to adopt them all. After seeing all those gifts, he couldn't blame Waffles if she wanted to live with Bentley and his parents instead of with him and their family. Was that even possible? Could a dog decide to switch families? Hugo had never heard of it happening, but he didn't know for sure. When they'd adopted Waffles, he hadn't been sure if he wanted another dog in the house, but now the thought of losing her made him want to howl louder than Waffles and Bentley had howled up the chimney.

Santadoodle, all I want for Christmas is to keep Waffles around!

Hugo took his drink of water and padded back to the living room just as the doorbell rang.

"Wow! The doorbell!" Waffles barked, zooming around the room even faster. "Just when I thought the playdate couldn't get any better!"

It was Mom. Hugo inhaled her familiar scent.

"We must do this again," Bentley's mom said. "The dogs are welcome anytime! We love them both!"

"Absolutely!" Mom said. "And Bentley should come visit us at our house sometime."

"Oh! Before you go," Bentley's dad said. "We made them some extra-special treats to take home."

She handed Hugo's mom two treats.

Jeez! Parting gifts? Hugo wondered. *Are they professional playdate planners?*

"Awww, look!" Mom said, kneeling down to show Hugo and Waffles. "They're shaped like you! It's Hugo and Waffles!"

Sure enough, one of the treats was decorated to look just like Hugo, and the other looked like Waffles. They'd even given her fuzzy fur made out of dog-friendly frosting.

"Who is that?" Waffles barked at the treat. "Who is that tiny dog? It looks like me! Who are you?"

Unreal, Hugo thought as he admired the details on his cookie's fur. He'd been in the kitchen when his own family baked Christmas cookies, so he knew how hard baking could be. These treats must have taken hours to make!

Mom thanked Bentley's parents and ushered Hugo and Waffles into the minivan, where they curled up in the back seat. Zoe and Sofia started arguing as soon as the van pulled out of the driveway.

"It's not fair! It's my turn," Zoe fussed, trying to take a tablet from Sofia.

"Dad! Zoe's stealing the tablet, and I'm in the middle of my show," Sofia said. Enrique was playing a game on Mom's phone with the volume way up. Compared with the gentle quiet of Bentley's house, the car was pure chaos. Mom was in the driver's seat going over everyone's schedules for the next day.

"Oh no! We forgot to get more wet dog food," she said, glancing at the clock. "But there's no time, Dad said he'd have dinner ready at six. I guess the dogs will have to eat dry food. Sorry, Waff and Hu!"

Hugo looked over at Waffles, who just shrugged it off. But Hugo hated eating dry food by itself. He sighed. His family was so frustrating—if they were too disorganized to remember to buy the dogs food, how could he ever make them realize that Waffles was about to have her heart broken? She was fine now, but it was just a matter of time. He knew that when she didn't get the Ultimate Ball from Santadoodle, she'd be a wreck.

And what if that makes her realize she'd be happier living with Bentley?

The thought made his tummy hurt. Or maybe it was all the treats. Either way, he knew he had a problem to solve.

CHAPTER 6

LULU STRETCHED HER legs and yawned as she slowly opened her eyes. She felt comfier and cozier than she had in a long time.

Who's a perfect doggy? Lulu asked herself.

I am! she answered herself.

And who had a perfect night's sleep? she asked herself.

I did!

It was the shark bed! This had been her second night sleeping in it, and Buttercup was right: It felt perfect. Lulu wished she could snuggle in it all day.

"OIIIINKK—shooo . . . OIIIINKK—shooo . . ."

Lulu turned her head toward Buttercup. She was still asleep, snoring loudly, and taking up most of the bed. They had snuggled most of the night, and then Buttercup had pushed Lulu a little over to the side by the morning. But Lulu didn't mind.

Loud snores were coming from the living room too. Human snores! Lulu craned her neck to see Jasmine's parents sleeping on the pullout couch. When Lulu visited their house in Minnesota, she'd never realized that they snored. But now that they were all crammed together in this tiny one-bedroom house, it was impossible not to hear it.

But even though there were two extra people and one extra pig in her space, Lulu didn't mind. In fact . . . she kind of liked it! As she wandered out the "ME door" (or, as some dogs called it, the "doggy door") and took her morning pee in the backyard, she felt happy to have these guests around. It turned out that Buttercup was an *incredible* snuggler. Lulu didn't even know that pigs *liked* to snuggle, let alone that they were good at it. But here she was, getting a great night's sleep and learning something new at the same time!

The morning before, Lulu had woken up so early for her shoot that she hadn't gotten to enjoy Buttercup's cuddles as much. But today, Lulu had a day off! And she couldn't have been more thrilled. Her schedule was usually so busy, it would be nice to spend the day at home with everyone. No cameras in her face. No assistants with walkie-talkies taking her lunch order. No pressure. Just three lovely people and one lovely pig. She took a deep breath, enjoying the brisk morning air.

Is this what it feels like to live with a big family? Lulu wondered. It felt wonderful to be surrounded by people (and a pig) who loved her, snuggled her, and allowed her to be herself and relax. *Is this how Hugo and Waffles feel all the time? I could get used to this!*

Lulu finished peeing and walked back inside.

Don't talk to me till I've had my pee! she thought to herself with a smile, and then she heard some banging in the kitchen. She followed the sound to see Jasmine's parents gathering things to make breakfast. Jasmine's mom pulled out eggs and bread, and Jasmine's dad put some bacon into a pan. Soon Jasmine's mom was whipping up some of the gooey stuff that Lulu knew eventually turned into pancakes, and the counters and tables were covered with tomatoes, potatoes, onions, and bowls full of things that Lulu had never eaten before but smelled absolutely amazing.

"Hey there, Lulu!" Jasmine's dad said as he adjusted some knobs on the oven. "Hope ya like breakfast!"

Lulu ran right over to him and licked his leg as much as she could. Yes! Yes! She loved breakfast. A mere glance at her Instagram grid would tell you that breakfast was one of her top three favorite meals! In fact, now that he mentioned it, Lulu remembered it was almost time to take her daily breakfast pic . . .

Just then, Jasmine stumbled out of her bedroom, rubbing her eyes sleepily. "Smells amazing," she said. Then she opened her eyes and got a good look at the kitchen, which was *way* messier than it usually got when Jasmine made their picture-perfect breakfasts. She looked surprised. "Oh. Wow."

Lulu usually took her daily breakfast picture at the kitchen table, sitting atop a tower of pink velvet pillows. But the table looked like total mayhem. Lulu watched Jasmine's eyes scan the room, looking for any nice-looking angle. Then she just shrugged and looked at Lulu with a smile.

"Morning, girl," Jasmine said. "Maybe we skip our usual morning post today?"

Lulu nodded. She had to admit, she was a little more excited about eating today's breakfast than posing with it.

"Okay!" Jasmine's mom announced. "Breakfast is served."

Lulu climbed up the tower of pillows to join everyone else around the table. Buttercup had wandered in, and Jasmine's dad scooped her up so she could be part of the family breakfast too.

"Must be nice to have a day off, huh, Jas?" Jasmine's mom asked.

"Yeah!" Jasmine replied between taking bites of eggs and patting Lulu on the head. "We've been so busy! It'll be nice to do nothing. We just have the holiday celebration tonight in the park, and that's it."

Lulu was an expert in Jasmine's body language, and

she could tell her favorite person was totally relaxed around her parents. Lulu agreed, it would be nice to have a day to just hang out and spend time together.

"And have you really given up on acting? Completely?" Jasmine's dad asked. "No more auditions?"

"Well, just to focus on Lulu, for now . . ."

"But you've loved acting forever, honey," Jasmine's mom said. "You've been doing plays since you were eight."

"I still love acting," Jasmine said, taking out her phone and typing in the passcode. "But right now, Lulu is a full-time job."

Tell me about it! Lulu thought. *I'm even more of a full-time job for me! Because I'm me all the time!*

"Someday you'll have to explain all of that to us," Jasmine's dad said. "I think we understand Instagraph now, but—"

Jasmine was staring at her phone now. "It's Insta*gram*, Dad."

Lulu laughed, panting happily with her tongue out and shaking her head. Sometimes older humans didn't understand social media as well as dogs did, but she didn't hold it against them!

"And the new show . . . ," Jasmine's mom started. "It's a show for dogs?"

"Well, it's *about* dogs. It's for people," Jasmine explained with a sigh. "People who like dogs."

"And it'll be on a website?"

"Sort of," Jasmine answered as she typed on her phone. Then she turned to Lulu. "Wow, girl, last night's post got so many comments! Maybe we should do *more* fairy costumes? I think we may have tapped into the fairy fandom. What hashtag did we use . . . ?"

Jasmine's mom and dad looked at each other, then back at Jasmine. As Jasmine scrolled through Instagram for longer and longer, their expressions soured. When Jasmine finally looked up a few minutes later, she seemed to notice. "What?"

"Well," Jasmine's dad said, "it's just . . . we came all this way to spend time with you. And I don't mean to criticize, Jas, but sometimes it feels like you're more interested in your phone."

Jasmine sighed. "You're right. I'm sorry," she said. "Just one sec . . ."

Lulu could tell that Jasmine couldn't resist. She started typing a response to one of Lulu's many fans before her mom chimed in.

"Hey! Maybe we could set a limit on phones while we're in town? One for all of us. We could use them for an hour in the mornings and at night, and we can capture any fun moments with Lulu and Buttercup, of course . . ."

Buttercup gave Lulu a smile and a nod across the table, as if to say, "Of course."

". . . but that's it," Jasmine's mom continued. "We have so little time together, let's enjoy all of it. No distractions, right?"

Lulu watched as Jasmine thought it over. That sounded hard! Lulu knew she was Jasmine's best friend, but sometimes she wondered if Jasmine's phone was Jasmine's second-best friend. Jasmine loved to post at least three photos on @LulusPerfectLife every day, at all the "optimal times," and she loved to respond to comments right away. But after thinking for a moment, Jasmine nodded and smiled.

"That's a great idea, Mom," she said, putting her phone facedown on the table and sliding it away. "A few days with a little less posting won't be so bad. It's the holidays, after all."

Jasmine's parents smiled and put their phones away too. With her phone out of the picture, Jasmine went back to eating breakfast with one hand and petting Lulu with the other. In between bites, she and her parents kept talking and laughing and catching up. And she tried to explain the new Waggo streaming app to her dad for the nineteenth time.

As the morning went on, Lulu noticed that Jasmine seemed a bit happier, warmer, and more . . . #present without her phone. Plus, it freed up Jasmine's hands to give Lulu some incredible ear scratches and belly rubs. And two extra people in the house meant four more person-hands! She was getting belly rubs *and* ear scratches *and* head pats *at the same time*. King sometimes called this a "four-hand massage." Well, right now Lulu was getting a *six*-hand massage. She felt relaxed—there was nowhere to go, nothing to do, no pictures to take. It felt great! Lulu wished she could post a picture right now with the caption "Enjoying a #NoPhonesChristmas!"

But that would defeat the purpose, she realized. *Never mind!*

"You know, it's a little chilly in here," Jasmine's mom said, standing up and walking over to her suitcase. "Now's a good time to give Lulu her early Christmas gift."

At the sound of her name, Lulu stood at attention and her tail started to wag wildly. *A gift? For . . . moi? After a nice pee, a delicious breakfast, and an incredible six-hand massage, this day just keeps getting better. I wonder what it'll be! Maybe a ball gown? Or a ball* and *a gown? A new designer handbag to ride around in? All of the above?*

Jasmine's mom grabbed something from her suitcase and walked back over to Lulu, holding the present behind her back. "Here you go, Lulu!" she said, revealing the gift. It was a puffy sweater. "Merry Christmas! I knitted it myself!"

Lulu's tail fell. It was the ugliest sweater she'd ever seen. It was a patchy mix of green, orange, and brown—Lulu hadn't seen that blend of colors since the time she accidentally ate a bunch of leaves and then threw up into another pile of leaves.

It looked like Jasmine's mom had *tried* to spell out "Lulu" in bright coral-colored yarn, but the last *u* was really tiny, so it just looked like "Lul," and it was totally crooked. Not to mention that Lulu knew coral hadn't been the color of the year in two whole years, so the look was totally out of fashion. Did Jasmine's mom think Lulu was color-blind? If so, Lulu didn't blame her. That was a common misconception about dogs.

Just because we can't see all the colors perfectly, Lulu thought, *doesn't mean we don't have taste.*

The sweater wasn't even ugly in a cool or ironic way like those weird shoes Kanye West made. It was just plain old ugly. But Lulu didn't want to be impolite. She had a discerning sense of style, but she was *not* cruel. So she licked Jasmine's mom's hand, then her arms, then her face to tell her, *Thank you! I love it!*

"Let's put it on!" Jasmine's mom said excitedly, and before Lulu or Jasmine could protest, she was sliding Lulu into the sweater.

Oh my DOG! Lulu thought as soon as it was on her. *This feels AMAZING.*

It was the coziest sweater she had ever worn in her entire life. Like the shark bed times a million wrapped around her whole body. Like one hundred wraparound hugs from Jasmine. What it lacked in style, it more than made up for in comfort.

Nothing wrong with wearing this around the house . . . , Lulu thought. *It's not like anyone will see it.*

Jasmine's dad put a matching sweater on Buttercup, and she too looked like she was in heaven. Buttercup's sweater had her name sewn into it, and the "Butt" was bigger than the "ercup," which looked a little strange. But Lulu could tell from Buttercup's smile that the pig didn't mind.

"Hey! We match!" Lulu barked.

"Aren't these the coziest sweaters ever?" Buttercup oinked back.

"They are!" Lulu said. "Mine feels amazing."

Lulu spent the rest of the morning—or was it the afternoon now? It was so hard to tell time without posting pictures every hour—lounging around the house. She sat on the rug, and then she sat on the couch, and then she sat on a chair.

Jasmine baked cookies with her parents, and then they all sat together and watched old holiday movies. There was a dog in one of them, and Lulu barked at it for a solid twenty minutes! That made everyone laugh, which made Lulu very happy, although she never got a good answer about whether the dog was actually in their room or trapped inside the rectangle.

Lulu felt strange. She was having *fun*. Or at least she thought she was. But how could she know for sure if she was having fun if Jasmine wasn't telling her how many views and likes she was getting? Her phone was still out of sight. *Is it really "fun" if nobody on the internet comments "This looks like fun xoxo"?*

Before she knew it, the sky was getting dark.

"Time to get ready!" Jasmine announced, picking up Lulu and walking to the closet. "We have to be at the park in thirty minutes."

Lulu was having so much fun, she'd almost forgotten. The town was holding its big annual holiday celebration in the park tonight, and Lulu had a paid gig representing Pet City. She basically just had to sit around, look cute, and meet her adoring fans, which were three of Lulu's favorite activities, so it wouldn't be too tough.

"Okay," Jasmine said, settling Lulu down on the ground. "We need to take you out of this sweater and put on your special holiday look!"

Jasmine took the scratchy star suit out of the closet.

You again, Lulu thought. She turned away and made eye contact with Buttercup.

"I think you should wear your awesome new sweater to the event!" Buttercup said. "Why not? It's perfect!"

She has a point . . . , Lulu thought.

"Why can't she wear her new sweater instead?" Jasmine's dad asked, echoing Buttercup's opinion.

"It's a great sweater," Jasmine said. "But Waggo wants to build a brand for Lulu by having her wear this outfit at all her public appearances. It sure makes an impression! Right, Lulu?"

Lulu looked at Jasmine, who was smiling and holding up the shiny, pointy star.

"Her sense of style and fashion is what makes Lulu stand out," Jasmine said. "And once our show debuts, it'll make Lulu famous!"

Well, when you put it like that . . . , Lulu thought, *she's right! My fashion sense is impeccable! And tonight is the next step on my way to being a huge star . . .*

So she let Jasmine take off her cozy sweater and put on the star. It felt even tighter and more uncomfortable than before—had it been in the wash? She barked loudly into the mirror, not only because the mysterious little Yorkie who lived in her mirror was barking back at her, but also because she felt so squeezed and awkward in the costume.

"You look GORGE!!!" Jasmine shrieked as she leashed Lulu up. Then she turned to her dad and explained. "It's short for 'gorgeous.'"

Hmm, Lulu thought as they all left the house together and started walking to the park. Normally, putting on an outfit like this would be the highlight of her day. It *was* pretty gorge. But right now all she could think about was getting home, putting her cozy, ugly sweater back on, and relaxing on the couch with her family.

CHAPTER 7

Grass! Stick! Dirt! Pee! Grass—SNOW?!

King pulled hard on the leash that Jin was holding, trying to get a better sniff of the white powdery stuff all over the ground.

"I think King likes the fake snow," Jin said to Erin, who had Cleo's leash.

King went to the park every day, but he had never seen it like this. The big field where he liked to play fetch with Jin, lie in the grass with Cleo and Erin, and take massive poops with his butt had been transformed into a total winter wonderland. There were ice sculptures! Fake snow! An ice skating rink! A big menorah with lighted candles! A kinara! A Christmas tree! All along the sides of the field were little stands where people were selling gifts and toys and drinks in cups that had steam coming out of them. King smelled *chocolate* coming out of the hot cups, which he knew was off-limits, but it still smelled amazing.

"Isn't this so cool?!" King asked Cleo, hoping she'd be just as excited. "Look at all this awesome holiday stuff!"

But Cleo just nodded slowly and looked away. She'd been in a bad mood all day.

"This is so fun!" Erin said. "They really went all out this year, huh?"

Jin nodded. King wagged his tail.

"All right, they should be waiting for us over at the dog run," Erin said. "You ready, Cleo?"

King knew that the agility program was having a demonstration, and they'd specifically invited Cleo to be part of it, since she was one of their star performers.

Maybe that'll be what gets her out of this funk, he thought as they walked toward the dog run. *Maybe performing will make her feel like herself again.* He was excited to watch her show off her skills.

But Cleo let out a long, loud whimper. She stopped in her tracks.

Erin looked concerned. "Cleo, what's wrong?" she asked, kneeling.

Cleo just whined again and held up her paw. Then she put it down and sadly rested her face on it.

"Did you hurt your paw, girl?" Erin asked. King was always very impressed by Erin's ability to know what the dogs were thinking. She lifted Cleo's paw to get a better look. "Hmm. I don't see any scratches or cuts."

"Should I take her to the vet?" Jin wondered out loud. Cleo moaned and looked down.

King walked over to her. "Does your paw really hurt?"

Cleo nodded but didn't say anything.

"Well, what do we do?" Erin said to Jin. "They're expecting Cleo to perform in a few minutes!"

Then Erin turned to King. "Would you want to do it instead, buddy?"

King's tail perked up, and he panted happily! *Yes!* It was an honor to even be asked, and maybe it would make Cleo feel better to sit this one out and watch him. Maybe this is how he could make up for the cheese failure and cheer her up.

King did some stretches to get ready while Erin talked to the people from the agility program. He guessed that she was explaining what had happened: that Cleo was hurt and King was going to run in her place. He thought they looked a little skeptical, but then they opened the gates of the dog run and it was time for him to show off his skills! Erin set King down at the starting line while some other humans gathered around to watch.

"You can do it, King!" Jin called from the other side of the fence. "You've got this!"

The whistle blew, and King took off as fast as he could. He darted around cones wearing tiny Santa hats and over ramps wrapped up like presents, jumped over hurdles wrapped with tinsel, and ducked under obstacles twinkling with tiny lights, while Erin guided him and coached him through.

What would Cleo do? he thought as he approached anything difficult. *She'd jump! She'd swerve! She'd run fast! Is that a leaf?! Wow! Cool leaf! No! Cleo would ignore the leaf and focus!*

Finally, he made it to the finish line and heard the sound of people clapping. He looked up to see Erin and Jin smiling proudly.

"You did it, bud!" Erin said, picking him up and rubbing him all over. "Great job!"

As she carried him out of the dog run, King noticed that the organizers of the event looked surprised and impressed. The man in the green hat gave him a thumbs-up!

Erin set King back on the grass, and he walked over to Cleo, who was sitting next to Jin's legs. She had her paws over her head and her tail buried between her legs. She looked sadder than ever.

Oh no, King thought, feeling terrible. *What did I do wrong?*

"I'm sorry!" King said to Cleo. "I just wanted to make you feel better . . ."

"Well, I don't feel better," she replied softly. "I think I need to be alone right now."

Did I somehow make her feel worse? King wondered. *Well then, I guess I just have to aim higher . . .*

King knew that one thing that always made him happier was gifts! And he remembered that Hugo had mentioned he was trying to find the perfect gift for Waffles. King thought that sounded like a very nice brotherly thing to do. And it looked like people were selling gifts all over the park as part of the holiday celebration. So, as Jin grabbed his leash and they started to stroll around the festivities, King looked at every booth they passed. *What would Cleo like? Little wooden toys? Finger puppets? A bag of candy?*

Then he saw it. Right in the middle of everything, next to the big menorah: the Christmas tree! It was really tall and covered with tons of bright lights and sparkly decorations. And all the way at the top was a big, dazzling, shining *star.* It looked golden, just like Cleo's favorite agility medals, but bigger and pointier and at the top of a super-high tree!

That's the perfect gift for Cleo! he thought, getting excited. *She'll love it. But it's so high up . . . How can I get it?*

"Hey, King!" Hugo's familiar voice called out from nearby. "Nice job over there in the dog run!"

King turned to see Hugo standing with Waffles and Lulu by the Pet City tent. Above them, Lulu's person, Jasmine, was chatting with Hugo and Waffles's family. Lulu's head was poking out of a costume that looked just like the star on top of the tree. Erin and Jin stopped to talk to all the people, giving King a great chance to catch up with his three best friends. Jin even dropped the leash to let the dogs sniff one another and chat.

"Hey, everyone!" King barked.

"You all have to meet Buttercup," Lulu said. "She's my new cousin. Or niece? Or aunt. Or something like that. She's a miniature pig!"

"Wow!" Waffles yelped. "She's so tiny, I can't even see her."

"No, silly! She's not here," Lulu said. "Well, she's around here somewhere. With Jasmine's parents. I feel bad for Jasmine; we have to hang out here because I'm doing this Pet City gig. Her mom and dad and Buttercup are wandering the fair on their own."

"Listen," King said, lowering his voice so that Cleo couldn't hear him. "I have a plan to cheer up Cleo. It's called Operation Get the Star from Way Up There!"

"What star?" Hugo asked.

"From way up where?" Lulu added.

"In the sky?" Waffles barked.

"I'm still working on the name of the operation," King said. "But basically, I'm trying to get *that* star from way up *there*." He pointed his nose toward the top of the Christmas tree.

"How are you planning to do that?" Hugo asked, always the reasonable one. "No dog can climb that high."

"But a cat could," Lulu said, with a twinkle of mischief in her eye. "I saw Pickle two tents over. Her owner is doing holiday paw-ticures. Maybe she could help. Probably not, though, knowing Pickle."

"That's a great idea!" King yelped. Their crabby feline neighbor with the anger management problem would be the perfect animal to ask for help. "Thanks, Lulu!"

"Did you hear me say 'probably not, though'?" Lulu asked. "That was the most important part."

"Hugo, Waffles. Let's go persuade Pickle to help us!" King said. "Lulu, I know you're busy here. Thanks for the tip."

"Um, I don't know if that's the best . . . ," Lulu started, worried. But King didn't hear the rest, because he was already walking off toward the paw-ticure station, with Hugo and Waffles following close behind. When they got there, they found Pickle lounging in a cat bed outside the tent next to a fuzzy striped Persian cat that King sort of recognized.

"Whoa. That's Lady Giggles," Waffles whispered. "Sofia shows me her videos on Instagram."

The two cats were sipping from fancy-looking cups filled with water while their humans chatted inside, not noticing their pets or the dogs who had joined them.

"Hello, *dogs*," Pickle said as King, Hugo, and Waffles approached. "Would you like a kitty-tini? You might not like them since they aren't filled with slobber."

"Nice one, Pickle," Lady Giggles said with a faint giggle.

Is that why they call her Lady Giggles? King wondered.

"We need your help," King pleaded.

"Oh, really?" Pickle purred. "With what? Stinking less? Sniffing your butt?"

"No!" King barked back. "I can sniff my own butt, thank you very much. And why would I want to stink *less*? Listen. I'm trying to help Cleo feel better, and—"

"I'm not interested," Pickle said. "Every time I help you dogs, it turns into a whole mess. Why don't you go give Cleo a dirty stick? Dogs love those, don't they?"

"Nice one, Pickle," Lady Giggles said, giggling once again. "Dogs, in my opinion, drool. While cats, you see . . . cats rule."

Hugo turned to King. "I don't think Pickle wants to help us," he said. "Maybe we *should* just give Cleo a stick."

But Waffles looked defiant. She took a step toward Pickle and barked, "Hey! If you help us get the star from the top of the Christmas tree, I *promise* that I'll put in a good word for you with Santadoodle."

Something Waffles said made Pickle change her posture. She sat up and stared behind the dogs, her eyes locked on the Christmas tree in the center of the square.

"He doesn't usually visit cats. Only dogs," Waffles continued. "But I bet he'd make an exception if I told him you helped us out."

"That's what you want me to do?" Pickle asked, as if in a daze. "You want me to climb that . . . big, tall, beautiful Christmas tree?"

"Yeah!" King said. "And grab the star at the top!"

"I love climbing trees," Pickle purred. "And I love climbing *Christmas* trees the most. They make the most jingly, jangly sounds. I haven't been allowed to have a Christmas tree in the house since the incident back in 2015 that we don't talk about anymore."

There was an awkward lull in the conversation because none of the dogs knew how to respond to that. It seemed like a touchy subject, and King did not want to pry.

"I tried to climb the Christmas tree," Pickle added. Then she stopped staring at the tree and turned back to the dogs. "I'll do it. That's the tallest Christmas tree I've ever seen. And it's just begging to be climbed. But let me make one thing clear. I'm not doing this for you. I'm doing this for *me*."

"Thank you!" King gushed. "Thank you, Pickle! I really owe you one."

So King, Hugo, and Waffles watched Pickle sneak off, slinking silently away from the paw-ticure tent and toward the big, imposing Christmas tree in the center of the fair. King glanced into the tent to make sure the humans hadn't noticed her walk off. Pickle's person was busy clipping a kitten's nails while the other human was picking out colorful polish. So far, so good!

When Pickle got closer to the tree, Hugo turned to Lady Giggles. "So, how do you know Pickle?" he asked.

"We're both cats," Lady Giggles replied.

Hugo nodded as if that answered the question.

"Look, she's doing it!" Waffles whispered. King

watched as Pickle hopped over a small fence and pounced onto the tree trunk, then scurried upward and disappeared behind all the decorations.

Then the tree started to shake! The whole thing rattled back and forth, and they heard a loud *hiss*, then an even louder *growl* come from the direction of the tree.

Uh-oh, King thought.

"Uh-oh," Hugo said out loud.

"Is the tree growling? And hissing?" Waffles asked.

"No, I think that's Pickle, *in* the tree," King answered as the tree trembled even more. By now some people had gathered around the tree, noticing the shaking.

"What's going on?"

"Is there something in there? Some kind of animal?"

"Or a ghost?"

"No, Debbie, I don't think it's a ghost."

"You never know, Suzanne. It could be a ghost."

"Debbie, enough with the ghost business."

The tree shook even more, and Pickle's noises grew louder and louder. Some decorations and ornaments fell to the ground and shattered. Pine needles rattled. Branches flew off. A couple of lights flickered and popped, and then all the rest of the lights on the tree went out at once. It was utter chaos! King watched as the beautiful, perfect star on top teetered back and forth, about to fall.

Oh no! Cleo's gift!

He rushed toward the tree, hoping to catch it, but he was too late. The star tumbled off its perch and dropped to the fake snow below. *CRASH!* It broke into several pieces.

Uh-oh.

Then Pickle emerged near the top of the tree and lost her balance.

She fell through the air and landed perfectly on her feet, with a wide-eyed look of embarrassment. All around, the humans gasped. Someone rushed to clean up the mess, while others stood around looking annoyed or upset, and a few just seemed impressed that Pickle had landed so gracefully on her feet. King was pretty sure he'd seen someone taking a picture.

"Pickle! That was you?" Pickle's owner ran out toward the tree and picked Pickle up. "I don't know what got into you. You are in a *lot* of trouble."

Pickle gave the dogs a look that King took to mean, *You've ruined my reputation,* as her owner apologized to the gathered crowd of humans.

"Oh no," King said to Hugo and Waffles. "We got Pickle in trouble. And for what? The star is totally broken! We can't give it to Cleo now."

"Look," Waffles said. "Part of the star is still in one piece. It may not be a whole star, but it's still really shiny and pretty."

Waffles was right. Half the star was sitting in the fake snow under the tree. The rest of it was broken beyond recognition, but maybe Cleo would like half a star? It was better than nothing.

King, Hugo, and Waffles approached the wreckage of the tree and each bit onto a different corner of the star fragment. Then they dragged it back to the Pet City tent, where Cleo was still sitting with Lulu.

"Did you guys see what happened to the tree?" Cleo asked, concerned. Then she noticed the star in their mouths. "Wait . . . Did you . . . ?"

"I goth you thith shthar!" King mumbled, with a corner of the star still in his mouth.

Cleo looked absolutely shocked and horrified. She stood up and turned her head away from King. "That's terrible! The Christmas tree is destroyed! The whole thing almost fell over!" she said. "I can't believe you had anything to do with that, King. I'm so disappointed in you. In all of you."

King laid the star fragment in front of Cleo, hoping she would see it and understand.

"I'm sorry," King whined. "I just did it because—"

"Because you felt sorry for me?" Cleo snapped, swiping away the star fragment with her paw. "Well, don't! I don't need your pity! I want to be alone!" Then she stormed off and sat underneath a tree.

"Hey, you did your best," Hugo told King. "It's the thought that counts."

"Yeah," Waffles added. "It's not your fault!"

"Thanks," King whined. "But if it's okay, I think I want to be alone right now too."

Hugo and Waffles nodded and gave him some space. King felt an uncontrollable urge to curl up into a ball and make himself as small as possible. So that's what he did.

Whoops.

CHAPTER 8

WAKE UP, HUGO! Wake up! Rise and shine!"

Hugo groggily opened his eyes to see Enrique in his face, rubbing him all over. Usually Hugo had to wake Enrique up and practically drag him half sleeping out of bed, but this morning was different, because it was Christmas Day!

"It's Christmas! It's Christmas!" Hugo heard Waffles barking from downstairs.

"Mommy! Can I open my presents?" Zoe's voice shouted from somewhere.

"Come on, Hugo, let's go get breakfast," Enrique said, springing up out of bed and running out of his room, toward the stairs. Hugo stretched and then followed him, letting out a big yawn. It had been more than a day since Operation Get the Star from Way Up There, or whatever King had ended up calling it. Hugo had stayed up late the night before, watching Zoe fall asleep on the couch waiting for Santa Claus and Waffles fall asleep in Zoe's lap while waiting for Santadoodle, so he was a little tired.

But the family's excitement was contagious. Hugo couldn't wait to join them in the living room. He was thrilled to hear Waffles barking happily. Maybe she wouldn't be *too* disappointed when she realized there was nothing in Zoe's shoes and that there was no such thing as Santadoodle.

When Hugo got to the bottom of the stairs, he smelled an undeniable, delicious smell . . .

Waffles!

Not Waffles the dog. Although he smelled her too. Waffles the breakfast!

In the kitchen, Sofia was helping Mom add strawberries and whipped cream and maple syrup to the waffles. Dad poured orange juice into five cups, then dog food into two bowls. Zoe was running around the house barefoot, waving a wrapped present over her head.

"I can't wait to open you!" she shouted at her present.

Waffles was in the hallway, sniffing around for Zoe's shoes. Hugo watched her find them and then look up, confused, when she realized they were empty.

"Huh," Waffles said. "There's no gift in Zoe's shoes. There are no gifts in any of these shoes . . . except for this dirty sock in Dad's sneaker, but I tasted it, and I don't think it's a gift."

"Waffles!" Enrique shouted from the kitchen table. "Come in here! We're having waffles!"

Waffles perked up at the sound of her name—twice—and she sprinted into the kitchen, jumping up to lean on Enrique's knees and get some really good pets.

"Here you go, girl," Mom said, dropping a big, juicy piece of a waffle onto the floor. Waffles ate the whole thing in one big bite. Everyone laughed. Hugo let his tongue hang out with a huge, gaping smile. It was hilarious. Waffles smiled and wagged her tail wildly. She loved it. Hugo remembered what it was like to taste waffles for the first time, so he totally understood.

"I'm. Named. After. THE BEST FOOD," Waffles barked, running in circles.

Okay, good, Hugo thought. *She's not taking the Santadoodle thing too hard.*

He walked over and licked her face, partially to say *I love you* and partially to taste any waffle crumbs in her fur.

"Some for you too, Hu," Mom said, dropping another piece on the ground, which he ate slowly, savoring every special bite.

Everyone scarfed down their breakfast quickly because the kids were so excited to sit by the Christmas tree and open their gifts. And as soon as they could, that's exactly what they did.

"Remember we have to pick up all the wrapping paper, okay?" Dad said. "Don't want Waffles eating that!"

Good call, Dad, Hugo thought. *I had to learn not to do that the hard way.*

"A pogo stick!" Zoe screamed, opening one gift. "I love it!"

"Whoa! A karaoke set!" Sofia said. "This is amazing!"

"Video games! I wanted these!" Enrique hugged Mom, then Dad. Hugo was pleased to see them get such thoughtful gifts. Enrique loved video games, Sofia loved to sing, and Zoe absolutely loved to jump up and down everywhere.

"And don't think Santa forgot about you two, Hugo and Waffles!" Mom said, turning her attention to the dogs. Waffles looked at Hugo and started shimmying her whole body with joy.

"Hugo and Waffles!" she barked. "That's you and me!"

"I can't wait to see what he brought you," Mom said, taking out a thick gift-wrapped present.

"Oh my dog!" Waffles said, jumping even higher, then zooming all around the room. "Hugo! It's probably the Ultimate Ball! Do you think it's the Ultimate Ball?"

Oh my dog, thought Hugo, *maybe Mom and Dad pulled this off without me after all.*

Waffles leapt into Mom's lap and tore open the package with her teeth. Wrapping paper flew every which way as she dug into it with her paws too. Hugo walked closer to get a look at the gift: two new dog-sized sweaters.

"Huh," Waffles said, her tail falling and her tongue going back into her mouth. "That's not an Ultimate Ball. That's not any kind of ball."

Hugo thought the sweaters looked pretty weird. Hugo didn't care much about fashion; he would wear anything Mom gave him. But they looked like the sort of outfits Lulu might say something lovably snarky about. Like, "Ew, Hugo, is it Halloween? Because it looks like you dressed up as an old nasty rug." He really didn't mind at all and felt that some old nasty rugs had a certain charm, but he *really* didn't want Waffles to be sad. He sniffed them and then rubbed his face against one. It was still weird looking, but at least it was soft. *Very* soft.

"These are much less itchy than the ones you had to wear in the pictures," Mom said, and suddenly she was holding the sweater open and putting it over his head. Dad put the other sweater on Waffles. Hugo felt the coziness right away, and he loved it. But Waffles wandered off to the corner and sat down, curling up into a ball.

Hugo followed and sat down next to her.

"I guess Santadoodle didn't come." Waffles sighed. Then she snuggled up into Hugo's side and looked up at his face. "I really thought that once I had a family, I'd get visited by Santadoodle at Christmas. But I guess not."

Hugo felt a pang of sadness deep down in his chest. Or was that some maple syrup from breakfast? Either way, he hated to see Waffles this disappointed. He desperately wanted to make Christmas special for her. So he stood up and walked off toward the hallway.

"Where are you going?" Waffles called after him.

"Uhhh . . . nowhere!" Hugo scrambled to come up with a lie. "Just going to the, uh, the bathroom."

"In the hallway? You know better than that!" Waffles asked, cocking her head to the side. "Good dogs don't go to the bathroom in the hallway, Hugo."

"Oh, er, that's right. Of course," Hugo replied. "You see, when I said 'bathroom,' I meant 'bedroom.' I have to go to the bedroom to . . . look for something. Be right back!"

Hugo ran out of the room and looked all around the front hallway for things he could stick inside Zoe's shoes.

Ooooh, a tennis ball! That'll work! he thought, picking up a tennis ball and letting it drop into a shoe. *Hmm . . . some lint? Maybe not.*

He found his blue moose at the bottom of the stairs and shoved it into Zoe's other shoe. Then he grabbed his Fuzzy Bunny, but when he looked up, Waffles was standing right across from him. He was caught.

"You don't have to do that, Hugo," she said. "It's okay. Maybe Santadoodle just couldn't find me. Maybe it's just because I wasn't officially adopted from the shelter, like Bentley was? You and Lulu and King broke me out before I was actually adopted. That's probably why Santadoodle couldn't find me . . ."

Hugo felt terrible. He suddenly felt like it was his fault that Waffles wasn't getting the Christmas she had dreamed of. Or the life she had dreamed of.

I have to fix this, he thought. *But how?*

"Okay, everybody!" Mom called out from the living room. "Time to go to Uncle Danny's!"

"Is everybody dressed?" Dad asked. Hugo heard the jangling of keys. "Sofia, can you get the dogs? Enrique, those are pajamas. Put on some real pants!"

"Pajamas *are* real pants!"

The whole place transformed into a whirlwind of chaos and disorder, like it always did right before the people left the house.

Humans! Hugo thought, shaking his head. *They can be loud and messy, but ultimately they add so much to your life.*

Normally he would run around the house, helping everyone get ready to leave. But today Hugo was too busy thinking about Waffles and how he could make her Christmas as special as she deserved.

CLOMP! CLOMP! Zoe was hopping around the kitchen on her new pogo stick.

"Mommy, can I bring my pogo stick to Uncle Danny's?" she screamed.

"Sure," said Mom. "But only if you stop using it inside the house."

"If Zoe gets to bring her toy, I want to bring my video games!" Enrique called out from the top of the stairs, where he was midway through putting on pants.

"You can leave your gifts here," Dad answered. "We'll play with them later." The kids whined in response as he seemed to remember something. "Oh! But that reminds me—Enrique, can you grab the presents for your cousins? They're in the closet."

Soon, Sofia led Hugo and Waffles toward the car as the front door closed behind them and the family poured into the minivan. Sofia held their leashes in her hand, but they weren't attached to the dogs.

"I want to sit in the middle!" Zoe said.

"Me too! I want to sit in the middle too," Enrique said.

"Same! Middle for me!" Waffles barked. Then she hopped up into the car, and Hugo followed behind her.

"Does someone have the Jell-O mold?" Mom asked.

"You're holding the Jell-O mold, Mom," Sofia answered.

"Oh yeah!" Mom said.

Suddenly, in the midst of the confusion and disarray, Hugo was struck with what he was pretty sure was a brilliant idea.

I know exactly what to do.

He jumped swiftly and quietly out of the car, onto the driveway, making sure not to be noticed. He watched as Enrique closed the door, and the van started to slowly pull away. As it left the driveway and turned down the street, he saw Waffles hop up onto Enrique's lap and stare out the window. Her ears were perked up, and she had a look of concern on her face that he'd never seen before.

"Hugo? Hugo? What are you doing?!" he heard her bark as the car drove off.

"Don't worry! It'll be okay!" he barked back, but he wasn't sure if she could hear. So he also gave her a big hearty tail-wag.

Okay, Hugo! This is your chance. It's time to save Christmas. For Waffles!

CHAPTER 9

LULU ROLLED OVER onto her back and let her tongue hang out of her mouth. She was so full of treats, she could barely move. She was still wearing her ugly sweater, and her fur was unbrushed and unkempt. She felt *amazing*.

"Buttercup, this is the life," she said lazily.

"Tell me about it," said Buttercup, snacking on some sunflower seeds.

Lulu looked over at Jasmine, who was laughing with her parents and playing a board game. The board game appeared to be all about wheat and sheep, so she couldn't imagine what Jasmine was laughing at, but she definitely looked happy. In fact, Lulu hadn't seen Jasmine that happy in a long time. She usually spent all day worrying about what Lulu was eating and wearing, emailing Lulu's sponsors, responding to Lulu's Insta fans, and scowling at stressful emails on her phone.

In fact, Jasmine often seemed stressed or sad or overwhelmed when she looked at her phone. But not today! Jasmine had put her phone up on a shelf after breakfast that morning and hadn't looked at it since. Lulu liked getting glammed up and being the center of attention, but she had to admit, it felt nice just lounging around in a comfy sweater with nothing to do.

Lulu closed her eyes. Today was going to be another great day.

Then there was a knock at the door. Jasmine opened it, and Lulu was shocked to see the whole crew of the *Hot Dog!* series standing there. She suddenly remembered that Jasmine had mentioned the crew would be coming over on Christmas to shoot what was supposed to be their "very fancy and sophisticated Christmas celebration." Lulu knew those plans must have been made before Jasmine knew they'd be spending Christmas with her family.

Oh well, Lulu thought. *I guess it's not a day off after all.*

Then she remembered how she looked. She was in her cozy sweater, and she was pretty sure she had "pig hair," which is the hair Lulu had realized you get when you spend your day cuddling with a pig. The crew couldn't have come at a worse time.

"Oh, wow, hey!" Jasmine said, smiling, but Lulu could tell she was caught off guard, and *not* too thrilled. She looked genuinely torn. "I'm so sorry. I totally forgot you guys were coming today! My parents surprised me, and I've been kind of distracted. We're having a sort of low-key Christmas, actually."

"No worries," said the director, pushing past Jasmine into the living room and taking a look around. "We can still make use of . . . whatever it is that's happening here."

"It's just, well, we're not really ready for a shoot," Jasmine admitted. "I'd have to blow out Lulu's hair and everything. Is there any way we could fake it and shoot our Christmas on another day?"

"Another day," a producer scoffed. "You can't capture the magic of Christmas on another day. We're not paying these people overtime to come all the way here and *not* get the shots."

Jasmine looked from the crew to her parents and then back to the crew again. "Okay, you can take some quick shots, but—"

"Fantastic!" the director interrupted Jasmine, clapping her hands.

Lulu groaned. She loved being on camera, but today

was supposed to be about eating, being cozy, and not moving. Now she'd have to take a bath and have her hair blown out and put that itchy star costume back on and everything. The *opposite* of not moving.

The director started barking directions to the crew. "Move this chair over there. Clean up all this mess. Find a way to hide the rest of the family. Except for the pig. The pig could be interesting."

The crew sprang into action.

"And get that sweater off Lulu ASAP. That's not her style."

"Well, what if that *was* her style just for today?" Jasmine asked.

"I don't think so," the director said. "Let's go with the star outfit again."

Suddenly Jasmine's mom was standing between Jasmine and the crew. "Uh-uh!" she said, wagging her finger at them, a stern look on her face. "That's quite enough of this. It's Christmas, for goodness' sake. Go home. Be with your families. And let us be with ours. I don't want to get in the way of Lulu's big career here, but some things are more important."

Buttercup oinked in agreement. "Yeah," she said to Lulu. "Some things *are* more important. Like snacks! I wonder if the crew would like to stay and relax and eat sunflower seeds."

Jasmine was quiet for a moment. Then she turned to the producer. "I'm so sorry. But we have to cancel. Can we plan another day?"

"Of course," the producer replied, frowning. "Totally understood. I mean, we did come all the way over here, on Christmas, with *allll* our heavy equipment, but . . ."

Jasmine's mom gave the producer a stern look.

"But of course we can reschedule," the producer added right away, in a voice that was a little too chipper to be real. "Not a problem."

With that, she turned on her heels and marched out the door. On her way out, Lulu heard her whisper to Jasmine, "But we really can't let this happen again."

The crew packed up and followed her out. Once they were all gone, Jasmine sighed. Lulu couldn't tell if she was relieved or more stressed. She knew she would have to get up close and lick Jasmine's face to find out. That was the best way to know for sure how someone felt and what they tasted like.

"Brunch is ready!" Jasmine's dad called from the kitchen.

As they sat down to eat, things seemed mostly normal, but Lulu could tell that Jasmine was tense. She was hammering her foot under the table and chewing her pinkie nail a bit, which meant she was thinking about something stressful.

"So, Jas," Jasmine's dad said, taking a big bite of eggs. "Should we watch *A Christmas Story* tonight?"

"I already told you I wanted to watch Hallmark movies," Jasmine said, but she said it too forcefully, like she was upset.

"Maybe we can watch *Home Alone*," her mom said.

"I just feel like I told you what I wanted to watch but you keep talking about how we're going to watch something else." Jasmine's voice was shaking.

"Jasmine, honey," her mom said gently. "What's wrong? It seems like this isn't about the movie."

"No, it's not," Jasmine admitted. "I feel like you guys don't respect the work Lulu and I are doing. You just kicked a whole camera crew out of my house before I could even deal with it. Sure, I didn't really want to work today, either, but it's going to make me look bad. I know you think it's silly and not *important*, but it makes Lulu happy. And it helps pay the bills."

"Oh, hon, we do respect you!" said Jasmine's mom. "And you know we love Lulu. We're just worried that you're losing sight of what makes *you* happy. My goodness, I remember how giddy you always were after performing in a play. All the way back to elementary school! No matter how small the role, you'd come out of that stage door beaming with pride. Now you just seem stressed and anxious all the time. You can barely look up from your phone. Even at the fair, you and Lulu had to work. It just doesn't seem like managing Lulu's career is making you truly happy. It was clear to me that you didn't want the crew here, and I'm pretty sure Lulu didn't, either. I was just trying to help."

Jasmine looked down at her plate and pushed her eggs around with a fork. She replied without looking her mom in the eyes. "Well, I don't want to ruin Christmas," she said. "So agree to disagree, I guess."

After the humans cleaned up the table and Lulu and Buttercup helped clean up the floor with their tongues, they all settled in to watch the cheesy TV holiday movie that Jasmine wanted to watch. Jasmine picked one about a woman who finds out she's a princess and gets married to Santa's nephew, or something like that. Lulu tried to snuggle up with Jasmine to cheer her up, but Jasmine was clearly still feeling a bit stressed, and she wasn't particularly cozy when she was in a mood. So Lulu snuggled up with Buttercup in the shark bed instead.

"Buttercup, can I tell you a secret?" she asked. Something had been building inside her all week, and she wanted to get it off her chest.

"Of course," said Buttercup. "You know what they say about mini pigs . . ."

"That you shouldn't exist?" Lulu asked.

"Well, yes. But also, that we're really good at keeping secrets. Anyway, lay it on me."

"So, I've always wanted to make it big and be a star," Lulu explained. "But . . . I have to say, I'm pretty relieved that we're not filming today."

"Me too!" Buttercup oinked.

"But what does that say about me?" Lulu asked. "About my life? Sometimes it feels like I'm on the express train to superstardom and I can't get off. I wish I could slow down, but how? And when? I don't want to let Jasmine down. She's my best friend. I love her more than anything. But it's too much sometimes. I know I could be the Elle Fanning of dogs someday, but at what cost?"

Buttercup sighed thoughtfully. "I think you've gotta do what's in your heart," she said. "The only thing that matters in this world is being true to yourself. That's why I like to dance to show tunes in my underwear."

"I didn't know that about you!" Lulu said. "I didn't even know you wore underwear!"

"Only when I dance to show tunes!" Buttercup oinked. "There's a lot you don't know about me. We just met! And you've been doing most of the talking. Anyway, if you're being your true self, Jasmine will understand. Because she loves you!"

"That's good advice. I just wish I knew what my 'true self' even was."

"You'll figure it out," Buttercup said reassuringly. "Just relax and enjoy the day. Sometimes the best way to figure something out is to not think about it for a while." Buttercup looked up at the rectangle and added, "Look! They're falling in love despite all the odds! Can you believe it?"

Lulu laughed. They'd watched three holiday movies already today, and Buttercup was still shocked every time the couple fell in love despite the odds . . . just in time for Christmas.

That pig, thought Lulu, *is too pure for this world.*

A FEW HOURS later everyone was dozing on the couch, and Jasmine's dad was starting to snore, when Lulu heard a light knock on the window. *What could that be?* She crept over to look and was surprised to find Hugo standing in her backyard! And he had a worried look on his face. She quietly slipped out through the ME door to talk to him.

"Hugo, what's wrong?" she asked, getting a good look at his outfit for the first time. "Aside from your sweater, which looks . . ."

Lulu stopped herself. The old Lulu might have made a gently snide remark, but she looked down at her own sweater, which was her favorite cozy thing in the whole world these days, even if it didn't score her any fashion points.

"It looks . . . comfortable!" Lulu told her friend.

"Oh no, is that a bad thing?" Hugo asked earnestly. "The way you're saying *comfortable* makes it sound like a bad thing."

"No!" Lulu insisted. "Look, I'm wearing a comfortable sweater too. Comfortable, ugly sweaters are actually the hottest thing right now. I love your look! Anyway, what's up?"

"It's an emergency," he said, panting. He looked determined. "I must, must, *must* find an Ultimate Ball for Waffles. Right now. Or Christmas will be ruined!"

Lulu wagged her tail. As someone who had spent the better part of her day being stuffed with treats and snuggled by everyone she loved, she knew that every dog deserved a perfect holiday. And if Hugo needed to make that happen for Waffles, she wanted to help.

"You mean you want to go on a crazy caper all over town to save Christmas and learn valuable lessons along the way?"

"That sounds a little dramatic," Hugo answered. "But . . . yes."

"Sorry, I've been watching Hallmark movies all day. Anyway, I'm in. Just one question for ya."

"Sure."

"Do we need a pig?" Lulu asked.

Hugo looked confused as Buttercup came trotting outside wearing the same sweater as Lulu. *If a pig waltzes through a doggy door, does that make it a piggy door?* Lulu wondered for a moment before snapping out of it and focusing on the task at hand.

"What's this about saving Christmas?" Buttercup asked.

Hugo stared at her. "Hi. I'm Hugo."

"Buttercup!" Buttercup oinked. "What? You look like you've never seen a tiny pig in a cozy Christmas sweater before. Now tell me, what's the plan?"

"OKAY, HERE'S THE last one," said Jin, putting one final gift in front of King.

They'd been unwrapping Christmas presents all afternoon, and King had gotten a giant bone, a chew toy shaped like a unicorn, and a big bag of T-R-E-A-T-S that Erin said would make his breath smell good.

Kind of a sneaky way to tell me I have bad breath, King thought, but he was excited to try them all the same. He tore open the paper on the last gift with his teeth.

"This one's for Hanukkah," Erin said, putting her arm around Jin. "But we figured, why wait until tonight give it to you?"

Inside was something so amazing and perfect and

incredible that King could barely believe his eyes: a brand-new Frisbee! King absolutely *lost* it! A Frisbee! He couldn't have imagined a better gift if he'd tried. Seriously, he closed his eyes and tried to imagine a better gift. He couldn't! King and Cleo had both gotten some really fun Hanukkah gifts the last few nights, including a squeaky fluffy dreidel toy that they had agreed to share, but this one was his favorite yet.

He started zipping around the room to let Erin and Jin know how much he liked the gift. They laughed and clapped, clearly pleased that he was so happy with it.

"Save some of that energy for later," Jin said, chuckling. "We'll want to take that Frisbee out for a test drive when we get back."

King spun around in some circles and then sat down. He was so excited that he barely noticed the sound of Erin grabbing her car keys as she and Jin walked toward the front door.

"Cleo, isn't it amazing?" he said. "We could play Frisbee! Me and you! Imagine that!"

Cleo shrugged. She'd been moping around all day and had barely cracked a smile when she'd opened her brand-new rawhide toy.

"I guess," she said, not even making eye contact. King sighed. It was hard to see her like this, and nothing he did seemed to lift her spirits. She was stuck in a rut.

"King! Cleo! We'll be back soon," Erin announced. "Just going to drop off some gifts at my cousin's. Stay out of trouble! Love you guys."

Then Erin and Jin were gone. King's mouth felt a little dry from all the running and jumping and leaping he'd just done, so he headed into the kitchen to get some water. He was taking a long drink when, suddenly, he heard a strange sound coming from the laundry room. He walked in and heard the sound again, coming from outside the window. He looked up and saw Lulu and Hugo standing on the air conditioner, tapping on the screen.

King hopped up onto a chair to get a better look, and to his surprise, on the ground below his friends, he saw a tiny pig wearing the same sweater as Lulu. King shook his head, certain he was seeing things, but Lulu, Hugo, and the pig were still standing there staring at him.

King pushed the window open with his nose. "What're you all doing here?"

"We're on a mission," Hugo said, not wasting any time. "We need to save Christmas by getting an Ultimate Ball. For Waffles. I know it's a lot to ask, but—"

"Sure, okay," King said. A fun day sneaking around with his best friends *and* a pig! No one had to ask King twice. He loved missions. Maybe they could call this one Operation Save Christmas by Getting an Ultimate Ball and Also Meet a New Friend Who Seems to Be a

Pig. And besides, Erin and Jin were out of the house, so nobody had to know! But right as he started to make his exit out the window, Cleo padded into the laundry room.

Uh-oh, King thought, *I've been caught! No way Cleo is going to let me get away with this.*

"King!" Cleo said sternly, and King thought he was done for. "I can't believe you were about to sneak out. Without *me!* Come on, let's go."

"You mean, you want to come?" King asked, shocked.

"I need to get out of the house," Cleo answered. "Plus, I never get to join your little adventures. They sound fun. Here, let me give you a boost."

Cleo helped King climb out the window, and then she easily jumped out on her own. Once they were outside on the grass, they started to formulate a plan.

"Okay, team," Lulu said, taking charge. "If we're going to get Waffles her Ultimate Ball, we need to be smart. I think the best place to look is the big pet store downtown."

"Genius," said Hugo. "Pet City. That's where I saw the Ultimate Ball first."

"Great idea," said King.

"Sounds good to me," said Cleo.

"So where is Pet City?" asked Buttercup.

All the dogs stared at her silently.

"I have no idea," Lulu answered.

"We always drive there, so I wouldn't know how to walk there," Hugo said. "I wish they'd let dogs drive. Been saying it for years."

"If it helps . . . ," King offered, "I know the pet store has a big sign and a parking lot outside of it!"

"King," Lulu said. "That describes literally every store."

"Right," King said, nodding. "I guess it does."

They decided to just start walking toward downtown, hoping they'd recognize the street when they got there. They walked for a little while, occasionally stopping to sniff a tree or chase after a chipmunk, and before they knew it, they were two whole blocks away from King and Cleo's house. They passed by Napoleon's house.

I wonder what Napoleon's up to today, King thought, sniffing the familiar grass of the Frenchie's front yard. He didn't have to wonder for long, because right at that moment, Napoleon came running after them. He was wearing a fuzzy blue-and-white sweater with tiny dreidels all over it.

"Wait up!" he shouted. They all stopped. "Hey, guys! It's so good to see my friends! And also a pig. Hello!"

"Hi," Buttercup said. "I'm Buttercup. I'm Lulu's . . . cousin? Sister? My people are *her* person's *parents.* Maybe I'm her . . . grandma?"

"What's new with you, Napoleon?" King asked.

"Ah, not much," he grumbled. "Just a little *bored*. My parents and Finn are all out at the movies and getting Chinese food for dinner, and honestly I'm a little jealous, but I'm working through it. I've got the whole place to myself, and I'm getting pretty antsy. Hey . . . wait a minute. You're all out on the street on Christmas Day . . . You're not up to some fun shenanigans without *me*, are you? Your trusted leader?"

Lulu quickly jumped in. "Of course not!" she barked without batting a whisker. "Why do you think we made it a point to walk past your house? We're going to find an Ultimate Ball for Waffles. By the way, do you happen to know how to get to Pet City? The pet store?"

"Sure do!" Napoleon said. "It's right near the nursing home where I see therapy patients. I always recognize it because it's got a big sign and a parking lot."

"See!" King yelped. "I told you!"

"Come on," Napoleon said. "I'll lead the way."

They all set off down the street after Napoleon, who, like he said, knew exactly how to find the pet store. They followed him, while he followed his nose, until they were surrounded by the bigger buildings of downtown. King thought it felt a lot easier than usual for this pack of loose dogs to weave their way through the city, since it was Christmas and most of the streets were empty.

“Here it is,” Napoleon said as they reached the side-walk of a big shopping center. King looked up to see the giant pet store. But all the lights were off! Cleo tried to rattle the doors, but they were firmly shut.

“Oh no!” Hugo groaned.

“Should have seen this one coming,” Napoleon said. “It’s closed for Christmas. I take full responsibility for not realizing this would happen and saying something sooner. That’s on me.”

Hugo whimpered. It made King sad to see his friend so stressed, but after trying some far-fetched schemes to cheer up his own sister this week, he totally understood.

“Now what do we do?” Hugo asked.

CHAPTER 10

HUGO STARED AT the locked doors of Pet City. They'd come all this way, but they were nowhere close to getting an Ultimate Ball for Waffles.

"Well, at least we got some exercise," Napoleon said. "Should we head back home? My family has some left-over latkes, and some of us have practice opening fridges. I know it's not the *best*-behaved thing to do, but sometimes it's healthy and important to treat your-self to—"

"Wait a minute," Hugo said, his brain racing for a new plan. "We can't give up yet!"

"Well, what do you propose we do?" Lulu asked. "The store is more closed than Lil' Stinky's DMs."

Hugo didn't have time to ask Lulu what that meant. He was too busy thinking. He had figured out one way they could get their paws on an Ultimate Ball, but he wasn't sure if it was a good idea. In fact, he was pretty sure it was a *bad* idea, but he needed to get that ball for Waffles, and so far, it was his *only* idea.

Any idea is a good idea right now, Hugo convinced himself.

"I saw an Ultimate Ball in the closet at Bentley's house," Hugo explained softly. "If we go over there, we might be able to get it away from Bentley."

The other dogs looked unsure. Hugo hadn't been sure how they would pay for the Ultimate Ball at Pet City, but he'd hoped they could figure something out. Taking a ball from a puppy, though? He could tell from their body language that they didn't love this plan.

"Listen," Hugo said. "*Waffles* is my priority here! Let's think about *her*! And plus, it's not like Bentley doesn't have enough toys. You should have seen that closet. There were enough toys for a whole dog-sledding team."

King and Lulu both nodded reluctantly.

"I guess if we're doing it for Waffles . . . ," King said. "And for you . . ."

"Bentley's parents like me," Hugo continued. "They said I was a good boy, a very good boy. If I show up at their door, I think they'd let me inside. If I'm a really good boy, maybe they'll even just give me the Ultimate Ball!"

So they set off toward Bentley's town-house complex and his fancy street that ended in a circle. Luckily, it wasn't far from Pet City, and Hugo remembered how to get there. As he led the way, Hugo thought he heard someone mutter that they still weren't sure about this plan, but he tuned it out.

They trudged through the streets in the chilly winter air. After a brief stop to hide in the bushes from a few cars and only two or three stops to pee (per dog, of course), Hugo recognized Bentley's block. The Christmas lights and decorations looked even more magical on Christmas Day. It wasn't dark out yet, but everything was lit up early.

"There's Bentley's house," he said, lowering his voice. "This way . . ." Hugo led the other dogs carefully and quietly toward the town house.

"Wow," Lulu murmured, looking at the elaborate, dazzling display in the front yard. "Are they on Instagram? Jasmine *needs* to see this."

As they got closer, Hugo heard some sounds coming from outside, and he could smell Bentley in the air. "They're in the backyard," he whispered. He walked over to the fence and looked through the slats, making sure he couldn't be spotted. Hugo was right: Bentley was in the backyard, lying on his back, laughing uncontrollably while his parents rubbed his belly. The other dogs gathered behind Hugo to look over his shoulder.

Bentley's mom got up to grab a treat from a table and held it in her closed hand while Bentley sat in place superbly, waiting patiently. Hugo could smell it through the fence—it was one of the incredible homemade treats he'd had the great fortune of trying during his playdate. Bentley's mom opened her hand, and while Bentley ate the special snack, his mom patted him on the head and his dad gave him a big hug.

It looked like Bentley was having the perfect Christmas afternoon. Enjoying his perfect yard with his perfect parents and doing a perfect sit and getting perfect rubs and eating perfect snacks. Bentley was the center of attention. Hugo remembered his own family's Christmas morning, with kids running around screaming about pogo sticks and pajama pants. It was Waffles's first Christmas ever, and it was total chaos. Gazing into Bentley's yard, Hugo couldn't shake the feeling: *That's the Christmas Waffles wanted.*

"What's that?" Lulu asked, nodding to the corner of the yard where Bentley's dad was picking something up out of a toy crate. Something round . . . something bright . . . something beautiful . . .

It was the Ultimate Ball.

Bentley's dad pressed a button on his rectangle, and music started playing out of the ball. It was another catchy song with *dog* in the lyrics that Hugo recognized.

Wow, he thought. *They can play their dog playlist through the ball? They thought of everything.*

Colorful lights flashed all over the Ultimate Ball. It was just like the demonstration in the store, but even better. Bentley's dad bounced it onto the ground, and on impact, it let out the most enticing *squeaaak* Hugo had ever heard.

"That's a really cool ball," King said, staring in a daze. Hugo watched as Bentley jumped up in the air and caught the Ultimate Ball in his mouth. He ran all around the yard, his tail somehow moving even faster than his legs. Now Bentley *really* looked like he was having the perfect afternoon.

As the furry little floof dropped the ball and his mom threw it across the yard, Hugo felt a strong, deep mix of sadness and regret.

Maybe Napoleon could sense Hugo's inner turmoil, because he stepped over and spoke up.

"What are we doing here, Hugo?" Napoleon asked with a knowing nod. "Are you really going to steal a ball from a puppy? That doesn't seem like you, buddy."

Hugo let out a long, deep sigh. "You're right," he said, turning to his friends. "I can't go through with this. I can't take that ball from Bentley."

"Okay, good," Buttercup oinked. "I don't know you very well, Hugo, but I was going to say, I don't like this plan. From the beginning, I was not a fan. You all seem like very good dogs."

King, Lulu, Cleo, and Napoleon all wagged their tails upon hearing "very good dogs." Hugo nodded in agreement. He didn't know *what* to do now, but he knew stealing Bentley's ball wasn't it.

"Sometimes acting rashly can fill you with regrets," Napoleon said. "I know from experience. Listen, I've stolen hundreds—maybe *thousands*—of balls from puppies, humans, and more. At my rock bottom, I stole a ball that turned out to be a very round turtle. And now that I've reformed my ways, I wish I could give back every last one. But most of them are chewed to pieces or buried deep in the earth, so that would be tough. The things

I've done . . . they keep me up at night, even more than the smell of peanut butter in the kitchen cabinet. Hugo, would getting that toy be worth the emotional cost?"

"No," Hugo said, shaking his head. "No, it wouldn't."

The dogs stared at Napoleon in awe.

"Wow," King said. "Was all of that written on a pillow on your sofa?"

"No, that was written . . . on my heart," Napoleon said. Then he nuzzled his nose into Hugo's neck comfortingly.

"I'm glad we could make this progress today," Napoleon continued. "My own growth is all about honesty and owning up to my past mistakes so that I can be a better dog and a better friend. Was I tempted by the idea of stealing that ball for a moment? Sure. And did I think for a second how fun it would be to take the stolen ball to the park? Absolutely. Did I consider that once I was at the park, I could knock over a hot dog stand, eat a bunch of hot dogs, run around frantically in circles for several minutes, and then chase a squirrel up a tree? I definitely thought that! Did I—"

Hugo cleared his throat.

"Sorry. Got carried away. Where was I? Oh yes. Even *I'm* not perfect," Napoleon said. "I'm still growing and learning. We all are. But I think we've taken a big step forward here, and I hope we can keep working through this together tomorrow at the park."

Man, Napoleon is good at this stuff, Hugo thought.

"The PARK!" King barked. "That's a great idea. That place is swimming in balls!"

"Not a bad idea," Cleo said, thinking it over.

"Sure!" Napoleon said, pacing back and forth. "We see balls there all the time. Maybe we could grab one that some dog left behind and forgot about. Sounds safe and ethical to me."

Hugo wasn't sure if that would work. What were the chances that someone had left an Ultimate Ball behind? Or, if they found a different kind of ball, that Waffles would like it? But it was the best idea they had, so he nodded enthusiastically. "Let's do it," he said.

And with that, the dogs and pig took off on yet another journey, back toward their neighborhood.

"Whew," Buttercup said, catching her breath as they finally entered the park. "I'm getting a lot of exercise today. If pigs could sweat, I'd be sweating through my sweater. Ohhh! Is that why they call it a sweater?"

"Okay, team, listen up," Hugo said. "If you were a ball, where would you—"

But he was interrupted by the sight of someone—some*thing*—zipping and zooming toward them. It jumped off a tree and scurried over so fast that Hugo couldn't even tell who it was until Nuts skidded to a stop on the dirt in front of them. He looked more frazzled than ever.

"Whoa there, Nuts," King said. "What's up?"

"My kids! My babies! They were *born*!" Nuts shrieked. His fur was sticking up in every direction, and he looked like he hadn't slept in a long time. He was talking a mile a minute. "They are healthy and they are good and Berries is doing well and let me tell you, mothers are unbelievable, how do they do it, I don't know, but *listen*! My kids! There's like a million of them! I don't even know how many! Do you know how many babies a squirrel can have?!"

"You told us it was seven," Hugo said.

"Well, it turns out SOME SPECIES can have NINE!" Nuts screamed. "And I guess we're ONE OF THOSE SPECIES! Or maybe it's ten? I don't know! I'm not sure how to count!"

"Okay, Nuts," Hugo said. "It's good to hear everyone's healthy. Congratulations."

"Mazel tov," Napoleon, King, and Cleo said in unison.

"But if you'll excuse us," Lulu said politely, "we're looking for a ball for Waffles."

"Can I help?" Nuts asked. "Things are pretty hectic, and I'm happy to step away from the nest for a couple minutes."

"Is Berries okay with—" Cleo started.

"I know where you can find a ball!" Nuts shouted. "There's a *bunch of balls* on the roof of the community center! Humans throw 'em up there and can't get 'em down. I see it all the time."

Lulu cocked her head to the side. “Nuts, how do you remember that,” she asked, “but you don’t remember where you bury your acorns every day?”

“My acorns! Where are they?” he gasped, panicked. “Oh no! I forgot! How will I feed my ENORMOUS PILE OF CHILDREN?!”

“Okay, one problem at a time,” Hugo said. “That’s a good idea, Nuts. Will you help us look on the roof of the community center? To see if there’s a ball up there?”

“It’s right across from the park,” King added. “You can be back to your kids in no time.”

“Of course I’ll help! Easy-peasy!” Nuts said as he scurried off toward the community center. “Follow me! Nice sweaters, by the way. You all look cozy. You know, they’d make great nests if you were willing to tear them into shreds for me. Okay, and I can tell by your faces that you don’t want to do that. Whatever. Come on!”

So the dogs and pig followed the frantic squirrel through the park and across the street to the community center. The roof was flat and pretty low to the ground as far as buildings went. The gym of the community center was only one story, but it was still much too high for Hugo to see what was on top of it.

"Okay, Nuts, focus," Hugo said. "We're looking for a big light-up ball. It's blue, and red, and yellow, and it has a lot of buttons and stuff all over it. It's really bouncy and really squeaky, and when you touch it, it makes sounds."

Nuts nodded along.

"But if you can't find *that* ball," Hugo continued, "then . . . I don't know. Maybe something similar?"

"You got it!" And with that, Nuts was off. He raced up a tree, then jumped from a branch onto the branch of another tree, closer to the building. He climbed even higher up in that tree, then perched himself on a branch overlooking the roof.

Hugo, Lulu, King, Napoleon, Cleo, and Buttercup sat on the grass looking up at Nuts while the squirrel scanned the roof.

Then Nuts looked down to them. "Good news, dogs! And pig!" he announced. "There's a ball up here that looks a lot like the one you just described."

The dogs all barked with excitement, letting their tails wag. Hugo relaxed all the tension in his body. Part of him hadn't expected this plan to work at all. But now they were close to getting Waffles an Ultimate Ball!

"Only one problem," Nuts said. "This branch is too far from the roof. And I don't see any that are closer . . . I won't be able to get it and get back down. And I probably should get back to Berries and my however many kids. I think it's eleven. You'll need someone who can climb up the side of the building to grab it for you."

Hugo understood and nodded. Nuts had been a tremendous help, but he couldn't do everything for them. He turned to the others. "Well . . . who do we know that can climb the side of a building?" he asked. "And who's friendly, available on Christmas Day, and willing to help us?"

"I know!" King and Buttercup barked in unison.

"Pickle, obviously!" King said.

"A spider," Buttercup said softly, but then she stopped herself. "Never mind. King's idea sounds nice. What kind of Pickle?"

"Pickle *could* probably do this," Napoleon said, looking up at the community center roof. "But do you think she *would*?"

Hugo shared a look with Lulu and King, then turned back to Napoleon.

"Only one way to find out."

PICKLE WAS SITTING on a cushion next to the windowsill when the dogs and Buttercup arrived at her house. They hid in the bushes next to Pickle's driveway so that nobody would spot them.

Lulu knew this was a long shot—her own relationship with Pickle was a bit of a roller coaster—but she thought of herself as a very talented sweet-talker, and if anyone had the skills to persuade this prickly cat to lend them a paw, it was her.

"You all stay here," she said, turning to her friends. "I'll talk to Pickle."

"Why you?" King asked. "Why should we stay in the bushes?"

"Because I'm an expert in persuading dogs and cats to do things!" Lulu said confidently. "Jasmine's friends like to say that Jasmine is a 'people person.' Well, *I* am a dogs dog! I'm sure I can be a cats dog too!"

"Okay, I'm convinced," King said. The others nodded in agreement.

Lulu held her head and tail high and walked over to the house, stopping underneath Pickle's window.

"Well, hello, *Lulu*," Pickle purred through the screen as she licked her arm. "Are you coming to ask me for another favor?"

"As a matter of fact, yes," Lulu said. "There's a ball on top of the community center, and—"

"I'm going to stop you right there," Pickle interrupted, lifting a paw. "Seriously, you dogs need to get your poop together. Maybe in a box or something. I can't solve all your problems for you. Well, I mean, I probably *could*, because cats are smarter than dogs, and more athletic, and better problem solvers, and better at listing qualities—"

"Okay," Lulu whined. "I get it."

"As it happens, I'm still in quite a bit of trouble from the other day," Pickle continued. "Thanks for asking. I see King hiding in the bushes over there. His last *genius* idea, with the Christmas tree? That got me grounded! *Me*. Grounded!"

Lulu turned and looked at King, who looked down at the grass, embarrassed. He could clearly hear their conversation.

Pickle went on. "Of course, I don't know if dogs are smart enough to detect sarcasm, but it wasn't really a genius idea. The opposite! *Un*genius. But I can't blame you dogs for having ungenius brains. I never should have agreed to it. I did do it for *me*, after all. That was my own bad judgment, and it was my fault I ruined the tree. I can own that. At the end of the day, was it worth it? Maybe. It *was* incredibly fun. I mean, all those ornaments with their jangly sounds. And their jingly sounds. I'm not going to sit here and tell you I wouldn't do it again, but NO! Not. Today! You and your friends need to learn how to solve your own problems for once."

And with that, Pickle stood up and hopped off the windowsill, disappearing into her living room.

Wow, Lulu thought. *So much for my powers of persuasion.*

She walked back to the others. "So, uh . . . did—uh . . . ," she stammered. "Did you all hear that?"

"Yeah."

"Yup."

"Every word."

"She's not gonna help us."

"That cat isn't very nice, huh?"

Lulu shook her head. "Looks like we'll have to do this by ourselves," she said. She wasn't sure it was possible. The ball was all the way on top of a *building*!

She looked at the others, who seemed just as discouraged. Napoleon and Cleo both looked like they were about ready to throw in the bone. Hugo, usually the one with the can-do spirit and positive outlook, was slouching, looking away from the others, with a frown. Lulu knew that this mission meant more to him than anyone else. Because it was for Waffles.

Lulu took a deep breath and remembered all the times in her life someone had told her she couldn't do something. Whether it was about her career, or pulling off a haircut, or just yesterday, when Jasmine's dad said he "didn't think Lulu could eat a whole plate of scrambled eggs!" She'd always proved them wrong.

"Listen up, everyone," Lulu said, summoning confidence from deep down in her soul. "There's nothing we can't do if we believe in ourselves and work together! We're five *brilliant* dogs and one extremely small pig who also seems smart. We can accomplish anything! Let's go get that ball, for Waffles. Who's with me?"

All together, Hugo, King, Cleo, and Napoleon barked enthusiastically. And Buttercup honked out a loud, determined oink.

"Let's do this," Hugo said with a smile. And they were off!

CHAPTER 11

How are we *possibly going to do this?* King thought as he stared up at the community center roof. *It's so high up! Did it get higher up since last time we were here? Is that possible? Did I get smaller?* He didn't think so. He was pretty sure it was just the difficulty of the task finally hitting him. He stood in a line with Hugo, Lulu, Napoleon, Cleo, and Buttercup, and they all stared up at the roof silently for a moment before Lulu spoke up.

"So here's the thing," Lulu said. "I was feeling all confident and big-inspiring-speech-y a few minutes ago, but now I'm feeling more run-home-and-go-to-bed-y. Doesn't that sound nice?"

"We're going to figure this out," said Hugo. "We have to! We just need a good plan."

"Don't worry," Buttercup said. "I've got this. I can jump onto the roof, no problem. I'm amazing at jumping. Check this out!"

Buttercup scrunched up her face and, summoning all of her strength, jumped about a quarter of an inch off the ground.

"Whoo!" Buttercup cheered. "Did you see that? I was flying! Tell me you saw that!"

"Buttercup," Lulu said. "Please don't take this personally, but you should be our lookout."

"You've got it! Happy to help. I have a very loud oink. I can let you know if I see anyone coming."

They all agreed that this was a good idea, so Buttercup waddled off toward the sidewalk to stand lookout. They didn't want any people, dogs, or both to come by and shoo them off before they could get the ball.

King and the other dogs walked around the community center, trying to figure out the best way up to the roof.

"Check this out," Hugo said, walking over to a small storage shed next to the gym. Then he nodded to a nearby trash can. "If we push that trash can next to the shed, I bet a dog could jump up onto the roof of the shed, and from the shed they could jump onto the roof."

The dogs all sniffed the shed, then sniffed the trash can. The trash can was empty, but it was still fun to sniff. They thought it over.

"Really?" Lulu asked. "You think that could work?"

"With the right dog, sure," Hugo answered. "It has to be a dog who's really fit, in great shape, super strong, and a great jumper . . ."

"Super agile . . . ," Lulu added. "Like, really, *really* good at agility."

All of their heads turned to Cleo. In this moment, King was so happy that his big sister had tagged along. Of course she was the perfect dog to jump onto the roof!

"Nope," said Cleo, slowly backing away. "Not me. Sorry, I can't do it. Don't have it in me."

She hung her head and walked away. King wanted to run after her, but then he remembered that sometimes when he felt sad, or anxious, or angry, or confused, or like he had to pee really bad but he was already in bed, or all of the above, he just needed a moment alone to collect his thoughts. Erin would often say, "I think King needs a *moment*." Then when he was done having his moment, he usually felt better. Maybe Cleo would feel better after her moment.

"What about you, King?" Lulu asked. "Can't you do it? Don't you compete in agility contests too?"

"I *do*," King said, chuckling nervously. And then he looked up at the shed. "But Cleo's the real star. I like to think of myself as more of the *comic relief*. You want people to be impressed, but it's also important to laugh, ya know? Now more than ever . . ."

"I thought you just won a fancy medal," Hugo said. "Weren't you bragging about it at Good Dogs?"

"Well, yeah," explained King. "But it was an Honorable Mention! And before that, I got runner-up for Most Improved! But the bar was really low. One time I got nervous and barfed all over the judge before I even started, and they had to take me out of the contest."

"That's still a big deal, King!" said Napoleon. "You *are* honorable!"

"That's right," Lulu squeaked. "And you *improved* because you worked hard and put in your best effort. And that's what counts. I believe in you, King! You can do this if you set your mind to it! Any dog can do *anything*—they just have to believe they can! And take charge! Wow, I'm good at inspirational speeches . . . I should play a high school football coach in a movie! And I *could*! If I set my mind to it!"

Hugo nodded encouragingly.

King puffed out his chest. Lulu was right! He *could* do anything! He just needed to focus, give it his all, and he could surely do anything he dreamed of. He let out a big, powerful bark.

"You're right!" he shouted. "I'm gonna do it! For Waffles!"

"For Waffles!" the rest of the dogs shouted. Then Hugo, Lulu, and Napoleon pushed the trash can over.

King turned and faced the shed. He narrowed his eyes and stared straight ahead, mustering all the strength he could. He tried to imagine all the dogs and doggy ancestors before him who had done amazing things—from the wolves who roamed the earth in packs thousands of years ago to Fudge the Poodle, who had a viral video where he successfully rode a scooter into a pool. He started running, faster and faster, and took a running leap up onto the trash can! Then he used all of his momentum to jump as high as he could up onto the top of the shed.

Yes! He did it. Or, he did half of it. He was standing comfortably on the shed now, but the jump to the roof was longer and scarier. He closed his eyes and took a deep breath, remembering what Lulu said.

Believe in yourself, King, he thought. *YOU. CAN. DO THIS!*

He ran off the shed and leapt into the air toward the roof of the community center, stretching out his body as far as he possibly could. His front paws landed on something, but his back paws slipped out, and now he was suddenly dangling from a gutter! Down below, his friends gasped. But he thought fast and swung his hind legs up and onto the roof! He scrambled to his

feet, stood up, walked over to the edge, and let out a proud howl. He'd made it! Hugo, Lulu, and Napoleon all yelped with excitement below, cheering him on.

Now came the easy part. King quickly located the Ultimate Ball and padded back over to the edge of the roof.

I did it, King thought. *I really did it!*

King pushed the ball over the edge with his nose, and Hugo caught it. But as King looked over the side of the roof at the dogs and grass and bushes below, he suddenly felt terrified. Was the ground farther down than it used to be? Why was everyone so tiny? He looked over to the shed, which now seemed miles away. He whined.

I can't jump that far! He panicked even more. *I'll fall!*

"Come on down, bud," Hugo barked from below. "You just need to jump back over to the shed!"

"Nope! No way!" King whimpered as he curled up into a tiny ball on the roof and tried not to look over the edge. His whole body was trembling.

Oh dog, oh dog, oh dog, what have I done! I'm trapped!

CHAPTER 12

"OINK! OINK! *OINK OINK OINK!*"

Just when Hugo thought the situation couldn't get any worse, with King stuck up on the roof and too scared to jump down, Buttercup let out some of the loudest oinks he had ever heard in his life. To be fair, he hadn't heard many oinks in his life, but still, these were very loud for such a tiny pig. And Hugo knew exactly what they meant: Someone was coming.

"I said oink, oink! Can you guys hear me? I'm oinking!" Buttercup oinked.

"Yes, we hear you!" Lulu barked back in a whisper.

"It's the pig alarm," Napoleon said quietly.

"People are coming, King!" Hugo called up to his friend. "Come down, you can do it. We're running out of time."

"I can't! I'm sorry!" King whined. "You should go. Save

yourselves. It's fine. I'll be fine. I'll just live up here from now on."

"That's not an option, bud," Hugo said. He hated to see King like this, but he didn't know how to help. "You've gotta come down."

Lulu turned to Napoleon. "Do you have any words of wisdom, Napoleon?" she asked. "Something from one of the pillows in your house?"

"Uhhh . . . ," Napoleon said, thinking. "'In this house . . . we always . . . drink coffee'?"

Hugo shook his head.

"Listen, King," Napoleon went on, trying to be helpful. "It's okay to be scared sometimes, but all you need to do is—"

"I can't!" King cried, his bark getting higher pitched as he quivered with panic. "I can't! I can't! I can't! I really can't!"

"What's going on here?" came a voice from over Hugo's shoulder. He turned around to see Cleo. She had heard King's terrified yelps and come back.

"Thank goodness you're back! Your brother got stuck on the roof!" Hugo explained. "He did a great job getting up there, and he got us the ball, but now he's too scared to come back down. Cleo, please. Can you go up there and get him down?"

Cleo looked up at King on the roof, with concern in her eyes. She thought about it for a moment.

"I can do even better than that," Cleo said. "I can *coach* him down."

Cleo walked right up to the community center building and stood on her hind legs, leaning her front paws on the brick wall. Hugo watched her look upward and lock eyes with King, then bark to him directly and supportively.

"You can do this, King," she said. "I know you can do this. Remember everything you've learned. When I first met you, you were this distracted and excitable little puppy. Now I guess you're still pretty little, and distracted and excitable . . ."

Hugo thought he heard King laugh a tiny, nervous laugh.

"But you're also *brave*," Cleo barked confidently. "And strong! And fast! And *kind*! Your kindness and your sweetness are what make you so strong! Think about everything Erin has taught you. Think about everything *I've* taught you!"

Hugo noticed that King stopped shaking. He nodded slowly. Cleo was really motivating him. It was inspiring to watch.

"The key to making the jump is to not hesitate," Cleo continued. "Plan your steps, push off the ledge as hard as you can, and aim for the shed. And whatever you do, don't look down. Never look down, King."

"I don't know if I can do all of that," King said nervously.

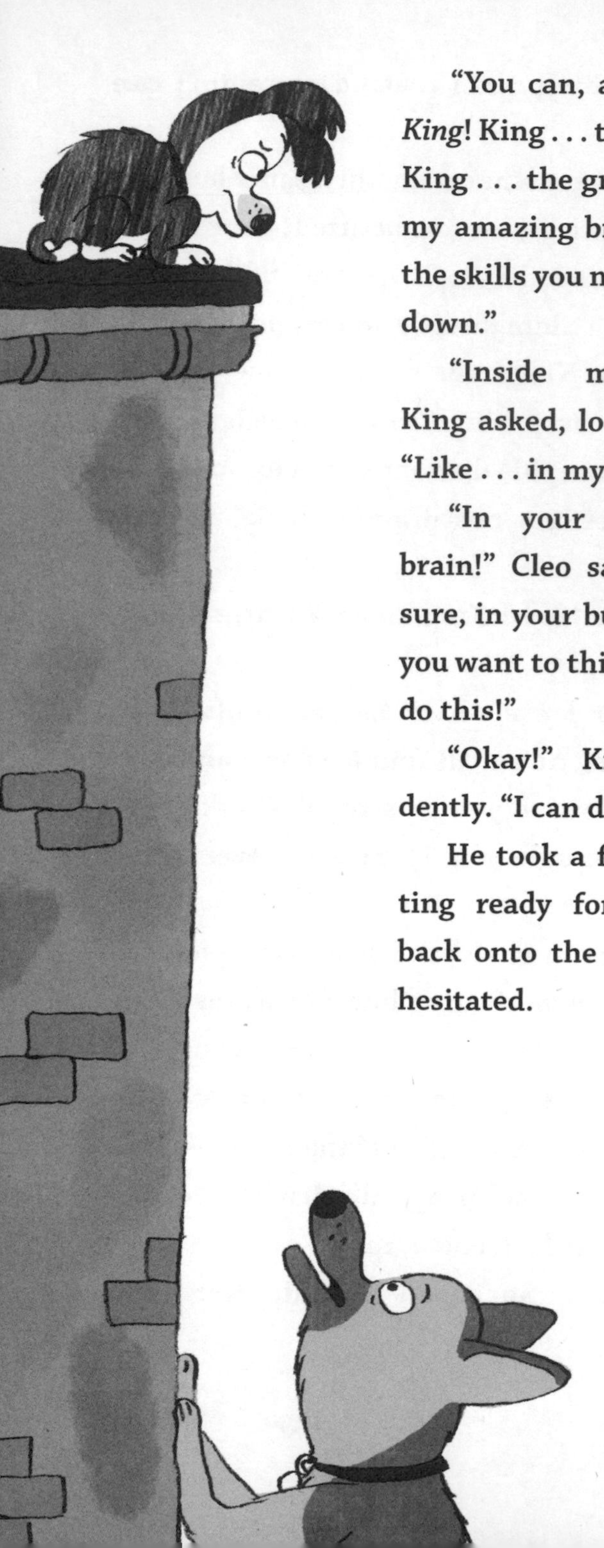

"You can, and you will! You're *King*! King . . . the agility superstar! King . . . the great friend! King . . . my amazing brother. You have all the skills you need inside you, deep down."

"Inside me, deep down?" King asked, looking up hopefully. "Like . . . in my butt?"

"In your heart! And your brain!" Cleo said, laughing. "And sure, in your butt too if that's how you want to think about it. You can do this!"

"Okay!" King barked confidently. "I can do this!"

He took a few steps back, getting ready for a running jump back onto the shed—but then he hesitated.

"Just a second," King said. "I found something else up here."

King disappeared for a moment, then returned with something tucked away inside his mouth. Hugo couldn't tell what it was.

"Come on, King!" Cleo barked. "No time for eating weird food off the roof."

"Itshnoth foods," King mumbled, his mouth full with whatever he had found. Then he positioned himself for the jump. "Okrrsh!"

"On the count of three," Cleo guided him. "One—"

And suddenly King ran as fast as he could and jumped off the roof! Hugo held his breath, watching King soar through the air—it reminded him of slow motion he saw in Enrique's favorite nature documentary—and then King landed feetfirst on the roof of the shed.

"Shorry," King said. "I don'th knowhowto counth."

"Great job, King!" Cleo said. "*Awesome* jump! Now you just need to get onto the trash can."

King looked scared for a moment as he peered off the edge of the shed to the trash can below. But then he shook it off.

"Ican dothish," Hugo heard King mutter to himself. Then King closed his eyes and hopped off the shed, landing perfectly onto the trash can. Then he easily leapt to the ground and ran over to join Hugo, Lulu, Napoleon, and Cleo.

"You made it!" Cleo beamed, giving him a warm snuggle with her head. "You did it!"

King smiled a huge smile, even though his cheek was still puffed out with whatever he had grabbed off the roof. His tail stood tall and proud.

"OINK! OINK! *OINK!*" Buttercup still had her eyes on the approaching humans. There were three of them, walking out of the park and crossing the street. They'd be at the community center any second now. "OINK! OINK! HELLO? HUMANS APPROACHING! OINK OINK!"

"Run!" Hugo barked as the people got closer. "Let's go! Fast!"

He grabbed the Ultimate Ball in his mouth and sprinted through the trees that ran along the sidewalk as the others followed. They were running as fast as they could, avoiding the streets and sidewalks so that they wouldn't be spotted. But Buttercup was having trouble staying quiet.

"OINK OINK! OINK!"

"It's okay, Buttercup," Hugo said. "You can stop oinking now. You did great."

But she couldn't stop. "OINK! OINK!"

"Shh!" Cleo whispered. "Someone will hear us."

"Sorr-OINK! When I'm nervous, I—OINK! I can't contr-OINK!"

"I can fix this," Lulu said, all business. "Hugo. Give me that ball."

Hugo nodded and dropped the Ultimate Ball. Lulu grabbed it with her teeth, walked over to Buttercup, and stuffed it into the pig's mouth.

"Hold this, Buttercup," Lulu said. Buttercup nodded, falling completely silent as they kept running through the neighborhood.

"Okay, we're almost at my house," Hugo said. "Time to give Waffles her ball . . ."

"We jusht needthoo make onequick shtop fursht," King said, suddenly veering to the left.

We do? Hugo wondered. But he went along anyway.

"Thish way!" King barked, and they all followed him down a street they knew very well.

Are we going to . . . ?

CHAPTER 13

PICKLE'S HOUSE?! WHY is King taking us back to Pickle's house?

Lulu was puzzled as she found herself in Pickle's front yard for the second time in one afternoon. King led them to the spot underneath the cat's living room window, where Pickle was back on her perch, looking out to the street.

"Psssht! Hey, Pickle!" King said with a muffled voice. Whatever he had grabbed off the roof was still inside his mouth.

"You again," Pickle groaned. "I *told* you, I'm not helping you!"

"We don't need your help!" Lulu protested, gesturing with her nose toward the Ultimate Ball in Buttercup's mouth. "See? We already got the ball off the roof. That's not why we're here."

"Oh. Huh," Pickle said, genuinely surprised. "You

actually did it. On your own. I'm reasonably impressed. So then why are you here?"

"Uhhh . . . ," Lulu started, and then she turned to King. She had no clue. "Yeah, King, why *are* we here?"

King opened his mouth and let a small ball fall out. It had stripes, and some little jangly things inside it. As soon as it hit the ground, it made a nice metallic clanging sound, like Jasmine fumbling with her keys, Erin getting their leashes ready, or the tambourine Lulu had posed with in that photo shoot where she dressed up as doggy rock star Stevie Licks.

Pickle perked up and stared out the window at the ball on the ground.

"I brought this for you," King told Pickle. "I found it on the roof."

So that's what he's been carrying around in his mouth, Lulu thought. *That's so nice.* Napoleon, Hugo, and Cleo also looked impressed by King's thoughtfulness.

"It's a ball that makes jingly sounds. And jangly sounds," King explained. "And I haven't tried it yet, but I'm pretty sure it makes jingly-jangly sounds too. I think I remember you saying you like that sort of thing? I'm sorry we got you in trouble the other night. But it's Christmas. And Hanukkah! And almost Kwanzaa! And I think it's a Wednesday too? All good reasons to give a gift to a friend."

Pickle hopped off the ledge and disappeared back into the house. Seconds later, the screen door on her front porch cracked open and she emerged. She glanced suspiciously over her shoulder, to make sure her person wasn't watching, then stepped onto the lawn and started swatting the ball around with her paws.

It rattled. It rustled. It jingled. It jangled. As it rolled around, Pickle pounced after it and swatted it again, trying to keep a straight face the whole time. Lulu could tell that Pickle didn't want to let on that she was enjoying herself.

"So you like it, then?" Lulu asked. "You like us again?"

"It'll do the trick," Pickle meowed. "And I'm *mildly* touched, if you must know. But my overall opinion hasn't changed. Cats rule. Dogs, as they say, drool."

"What about pigs?" Buttercup dropped the Ultimate Ball to ask.

"I have no opinion about pigs," Pickle said coldly.

"Ouch, even worse," Buttercup said softly. "Oh, well. The holidays are about giving, not getting. You have a blessed day, ma'am."

Buttercup turned to leave, and Lulu followed, with all the other dogs close behind. Lulu had been impressed by King's athletic and acrobatic leap onto the roof and back onto the shed. But somehow she was even more impressed that he'd thought to bring Pickle such a lovely gift.

"That was so sweet of you, King," Cleo said. "I'm proud."

"A real mitzvah," Napoleon added. "I'm proud of all of us today."

They held their heads high as they walked away from Pickle's house.

A LITTLE WHILE later, after two or three pee stops and one or two stick sniffs, Lulu was sitting in Hugo's backyard with the others, waiting for Waffles to come back home with the rest of Hugo's family. Hugo had already placed the Ultimate Ball in one of Zoe's slippers inside the house.

Just as Lulu was starting to yawn from a long and

very eventful day, she was jolted alert by the sound of a car pulling into the driveway on the other side of the house.

"They're home! They're home!" Hugo barked. They all turned eagerly to the tall glass doors by the patio, where they had a good view into Hugo's living room. Lulu, King, Cleo, Napoleon, and Buttercup hid behind some potted plants so that none of the people in Hugo's family would notice that all the neighborhood dogs (and pig) were in their backyard for some reason.

Lulu watched as his family came inside. Some of them sat on the couch, others went upstairs, and Hugo's dad went into the kitchen. But Waffles noticed Zoe's slipper right away and ran over to it. As soon as she got up close and saw the Ultimate Ball, her eyes lit up. Her entire body started wiggling and wagging with delight. She picked up the ball in her mouth and looked out the window, noticing Hugo on the patio. Waffles walked out the doggy door. Lulu and the others emerged from their hiding spaces to sniff her hello.

Waffles dropped the ball from her mouth and sniffed her brother all over to make sure he was okay. "Where did you go?!" she asked Hugo, concerned. "Everyone got so worried when they realized you weren't in the car! But we were already halfway there, and they figured they had left you in the house, so it was okay.

Did you see? Did everybody see? Santadoodle came! Santadoodle came!"

She picked up the ball again and did a little dance in a little circle. Hugo smiled. Then she dropped it again to talk.

"It's the Ultimate Ball!" Waffles said. "But I feel bad . . . Did Santadoodle bring you anything, Hugo? In Enrique's shoe?"

"I got everything I needed this Christmas," Hugo nodded, licking Waffles's face. "Let's go play with that ball."

Waffles took the Ultimate Ball to the grass, and everyone followed her. She nudged it with her nose, then bit it with her teeth, then tapped it with her paw. "Huh," she said. "It doesn't light up or make any noise . . ."

"Uh-oh," Cleo said. "The batteries must be dead. It was up on the roof for so long—I mean, it was in Santadoodle's bag for so long?"

"Oh no!" Hugo cried. He looked devastated. "I'm so sorry, Waffles!"

"It's okay!" Waffles said. "It's still fun! Look!"

Waffles kicked the ball across the yard, then sprinted after it and caught it in her mouth while doing a full body roll. "See?" Waffles barked excitedly. Then she sniffed the ball and licked it, wiggling her whole body gleefully. "I love it! I love it even more than the one from the store, because this one smells like my best friends! And also a pig?"

"Hi! I'm Buttercup!" Buttercup said.

"I'm Waffles!" Waffles gave Buttercup a big sniff hello before turning back to Hugo. "And not to mention, this ball is *mine*, and that makes it the perfect gift. This is the perfect Christmas!"

Hugo's whole body relaxed, and he let out a huge, floppy-tongued, smile. Lulu felt great to see both

Waffles and Hugo so happy. King ran over and played with the ball with Waffles, then Napoleon joined, and pretty soon all the dogs and Buttercup were in a big pile in the middle of the grass, rolling around, passing the ball back and forth, and laughing. Lulu joined in the dog pile, and it suddenly occurred to her that if Jasmine were there taking pictures, they'd have Instagram *gold.* Or it would make an incredible scene for her reality show! But actually . . . she realized it was even better to have the moment all to themselves and not always be waiting for the comments to roll in.

Maybe some experiences don't need to be pictures, Lulu thought. *They can just be memories.*

"Lulu!" Waffles barked. "It's so nice to wrestle with you! You're not worried about your haircut? Or your *moneymaker*?"

"Not today," Lulu answered. "Right now all I'm worried about is having a good time."

After a few glorious grassy tumbles and a couple of rounds of a new game King and Waffles invented called Bite the Ball as Hard as You Can, Lulu started to feel a bit of a chill, even through her toasty sweater, and she looked up and noticed that the sun was getting lower in the sky.

"Well," she said to the others, "I think Buttercup and I had better head home, before Jasmine and her parents realize we're gone. This has been lovely."

"We have to go too," Cleo said. "Come on, King. Erin and Jin are probably on their way back by now."

King nodded and stood to leave. "Wow." He sighed happily. "I can't believe one broken ball gave us all so much fun for a whole afternoon."

"A real Hanukkah miracle," Cleo agreed.

"I'll probably hit the road too," Napoleon said. "Another thrilling adventure in the books. Thanks for inviting me. And remember, home is where the heart is, so dance like nobody is watching and *always* kiss the cook!"

"Happy holidays, everyone!" Buttercup barked over her shoulder as she and Lulu walked out through the gate. "What a thrill it was to meet all of Lulu's best friends!"

CHAPTER 14

IT WAS DARK outside the windows now, and King was pooped. He snuggled up on the couch with Cleo, resting his head on her back, and felt like he might let his eyes close for a little pre-dinner nap . . .

Yeah, that's a nice idea, he thought. *Then I'll be well rested for dinner and my post-dinner nap . . .*

But then he remembered something. He stood up. "Cleo!" King nudged her. "I almost forgot. I have a present for you!"

King hopped off the couch and trotted across the room to the end table, where his Honorable Mention medal was sitting in all its shiny, shiny glory. He picked it up and brought it back over to the couch.

"This is for you," he said, placing the medal on the couch next to Cleo's surprised face.

"I thought you loved this medal," she said. "It means so much to you."

"I do. And it does," he said. "But you deserve it more than I do. I might have been an Honorable Mention, but *you're* the reason I'm both honorable and mentioned. You're the best coach and big sister a dog could have."

Cleo leaned over to nuzzle him. "Thanks, bud," she said. "But you can keep the medal. You earned it. Your friendship is worth more to me than any award. And maybe you're right. Coaching you reminded me that I have much more to offer than just my agility skills. Which are still phenomenal, by the way. I shouldn't be too hard on myself."

Cleo rolled onto her side, inviting King in for a big wraparound cuddle, which felt unbelievable. After seeing all his friends in goofy but amazingly cozy-looking sweaters all day, he thought he might know what they felt like . . .

Cleo is my sweater! he thought as he let her fur warm him up. *Cleo is the best sweater!* And for

the first time all week, King didn't feel worried about Cleo. He knew she was going to be okay.

"Awww!" Jin said as he walked into the living room with a mug of hot chocolate and some matches for the Hanukkah candles. "Babe, look, they're snuggling."

Erin ran in and snapped a picture of King wrapped up in Cleo's arms. King hoped Erin and Jin would come over to the couch and give them some pets. Maybe some rubs. A scratch? That would be the best: his perfectly sized family of four relaxing on the couch together, celebrating Christmas night and the end of Hanukkah.

"Ooooh!" Erin cooed. "They're so sweet. It's good to see them getting along so well and being so well behaved, since our family is about to get bigger."

HUH?! King looked at Cleo, confused. She seemed just as shocked as he was.

"Cleo???" King asked. "How does a *family* get *bigger*? Erin and Jin are already so much taller than us, and I feel like *I'm* a good size, and I don't really want to get bigger. Will we have to go inside some kind of machine or—"

Cleo just looked startled and waited for Erin to say more.

"King. Cleo," Erin gushed with a smile. "We're having a baby!"

Oh. No.

King almost fell off the couch.

Hugo

HUGO SAT ON the rug with Waffles, rolling the Ultimate Ball back and forth. Mom and Dad cleaned the dishes from dinner, and the kids played with Enrique's new video games on the couch. It had been a long, exhausting day, so it felt nice to wind down and relax.

Ding-dong!

Hugo sat up and stood at attention, like he did every time he heard the doorbell ring. Waffles ran around the coffee table in circles like she did anytime she heard any noise.

"Who could that be?" Hugo asked.

"Probably the doorbell," Waffles said. "But what's the doorbell doing here?"

"No, I mean, who's *at* the . . . Ah, never mind."

Mom walked over and opened the door. To Hugo's surprise, it was *Bentley*! And Bentley's parents! And Bentley was wearing a *very* elaborate Santa Claus costume, with a red jacket, red hat, and white "hair" hanging off his chin.

"Wow, what a nice surprise!" Mom said. "And I love that costume; he looks adorable."

Waffles took one look at Bentley and froze in place with her tongue hanging out.

"Oh. My. Dog," she muttered. "Hugo. Psst. Look. It's Santadoodle."

Hugo looked at Waffles, then at Bentley in his Santa outfit, and then back at Waffles. Did she think *Bentley* was *Santadoodle*?

"Hey, Waffles!" Bentley barked.

"He. Knows. My. Name!" Waffles shrieked. "Of course he does! Wowowowowowow!"

Waffles was so excited that she must not have noticed Bentley's parents or heard them talking.

"We're so sorry for dropping by unannounced," Bentley's mom said. "But we're about to visit some of our family in the neighborhood, and we wanted to drop off a gift for Waffles."

Bentley's dad took out a brand-new Ultimate Ball and handed it to Hugo's mom. It was still in its packaging, in perfect condition.

"Wow! Thank you so much!" Mom said as she opened the box. Then she walked over to Waffles. "Hey, girl, look what you just got!"

Mom set the Ultimate Ball on the ground, and Waffles's eyes lit up. So did all the lights on the ball. It worked flawlessly, unlike the one Hugo had brought back for her. Hugo's tail fell between his legs.

Oh no, he thought, watching Bentley and Waffles play together with the brand-new Ultimate Ball. *Bentley's family gave Waffles her biggest wish, and our family didn't even know she* had *a biggest wish . . .*

"Hey, Waffles, c'mere," he said softly, walking into the corner of the kitchen to speak to her alone. She followed him. He hung his head sadly, unsure how to say what he was thinking.

"Look, I know this hasn't been the Christmas you dreamed of, and . . . well, I know you have *options*. Whatever you want to do, I understand," he mumbled.

"Huh? What are you talking about?" Waffles asked.

"If you want to go live with Bentley and his family instead of us," Hugo said, "I'd get it. They love you, and they brought you what you wanted for Christmas. I love you too, we all do, but Bentley's family really *gets* you, don't they?"

"Don't be silly," Waffles said, baffled. "Sure, Santadoodle brought me my biggest wish, but it wasn't the Ultimate Ball. My biggest wish was to find my family, and I did! It's Zoe, and you, and Mom and Dad and Enrique and the older girl."

"Sofia."

"Right, I always forget that one. Yeah, I was excited to find Bentley. Of course I was! But *this* is my home. Forever!"

She rubbed her head into Hugo's chin and licked his face. Hugo felt relieved. Thank goodness Waffles didn't want to go live anywhere else! He had to admit he was getting pretty attached to her.

"Come on, let's play!" Waffles said. "If only Bentley were here to see all this . . . I wonder why they didn't bring him!"

She led Hugo back into the living room, where Bentley, aka Fuzzface, aka Santadoodle, was waiting.

"Now I have one Ultimate Ball for inside and one for the yard! I'm the luckiest puppy!" She looked right at Bentley. "Thank you, Santadoodle!" Waffles howled.

Bentley turned to Hugo. "Uhh, does she think *I'm*—?"

"Shh," Hugo said. "Let her have this."

So the three dogs played with the Ultimate Ball while Mom invited Bentley's parents into the kitchen, Dad brought out cookies and made hot chocolate, and the kids played on the couch. Then Zoe lay down on the floor and let the dogs climb all over her and lick her face.

It had turned into a perfect night.

CHAPTER 15

LULU SNUGGLED DEEPER into Jasmine's lap. They were in the back of a taxi, sitting between Jasmine's parents, on their way downtown for a New Year's Eve party. And not just any New Year's Eve party. This was a party *for dogs*—all the fanciest dog influencers would be there, with their owners as "plus ones." And Lulu was the host. As they pulled up to the event space, which was the outdoor back patio of an upscale restaurant, she saw the balloons and signs: "Lulu's Perfect Barkin' New Year's Eve."

Lulu was a little nervous as they got out of the cab. The *Hot Dog!* film crew would be here tonight, filming Lulu for the series, and this was the first time she would see them since Christmas Day, when Jasmine's mom had asked them to leave.

"I'm sorry to drag you guys to this," Jasmine told her parents. "I got a pretty sternly worded email from the production company. They really want to keep to the schedule from now on."

"It's no problem at all, honey," Jasmine's mom said as they walked into the outdoor party area. "It'll be fun! Wow, this is *fancy*."

Jasmine's mom was right. It *was* fancy. All the most famous Instagram dogs were there, and even some dogs from TikTok. There was a doggy DJ, a poodle ice sculpture, and a dog-friendly specialty "cock(er spaniel) tail" made from chicken soup. Some dogs and their owners were wearing matching tuxedos. Lulu, meanwhile, was wearing her new favorite cozy homemade sweater. It was an outdoor party in the cold, so why wouldn't she? In fact, she'd been wearing it most of the week since her big Christmas adventure. Jasmine had tried a few times to get Lulu into something more festive, but each time, Lulu had whined and Jasmine had respected Lulu's wishes to stay in her ugly lumpy sweater. She hoped the people at the party would let her keep it on.

The old Lulu from a week ago would have *loved* a party like this. It would have been a

chance to see and be seen, sniff and be sniffed! But the new Lulu just wanted to curl up on Jasmine's lap at home and watch the ball drop in the square on the rectangle. She was jealous of Buttercup, who was at home by herself, snuggled up in her shark bed. Lulu wished she were there too. Instead, she had to stand outside all night in the cold, greeting guests and hamming it up for the camera.

What a life, thought Lulu. *I wonder if Meryl Streep ever had to film a web series she didn't want to.*

As soon as they got to the center of the party, the film crew swarmed around her. They started poking at her fur, showing her where to stand, how to stand, what to do. Then a stylist pulled out the dreaded star costume. *Not again,* thought Lulu. This pointy, itchy costume was following her everywhere! Someone had glammed it up with little rhinestones and some huge glasses with numbers on them for New Year's, but the whole thing looked just as uncomfortable as ever. Lulu remembered that the star felt too hot when she was inside and too cold when she was outside at the festival in the park. It wasn't right for any weather, and Lulu shivered just thinking about it. The on-set hairstylist walked over, holding a can of . . . something.

"What's that?" Jasmine asked.

"Silver hairspray!" the hairstylist said, shaking the can. "Jasmine, can you cover Lulu's eyes for me? I have *no idea* what's in this stuff."

"And let's get her out of that sweater!" the wardrobe assistant shouted.

Easy for you to say, lady! Lulu thought, taking a few steps back and looking at the assistant's puffy coat, hat, gloves, and scarf.

Suddenly Lulu realized something: She didn't want any of this! She didn't want the dress, or the hair, or the fancy party. She didn't even want the photo booth where you could make it look like Lil' Stinky was farting on you. She just wanted to be home with her family, watching terrible movies and eating too many snacks. Sure, she loved fashion and parties, but on her own terms.

Lulu knew that fashion was all about showing off your true self to the world. Well, what if tonight, her true self wanted to be cozy and relaxed? Then her sweater was fashionable, right? She remembered what Buttercup had said: *If you're being your true self, Jasmine will understand.* Tonight she wasn't feeling like a fancy dress, and it was time to do something about it.

"Come on, girl, let's get you out of this sweater," Jasmine was saying.

Lulu whimpered and let out a yelp. She pressed her

paws into her sleeves and bit onto the collar so that nobody could remove the sweater.

Jasmine looked at her, surprised. "What is it, girl?"

Lulu looked up at Jasmine and tried as hard as she could to say, *I'm sorry, but I don't want to* with her eyes.

"I think I get it," said Jasmine, rubbing Lulu's head affectionately with a knowing look. "But we came all the way here. I think we can still make it work."

Jasmine turned to the producer. "I don't think Lulu wants to wear the costume," she explained. "Maybe she can keep her sweater on but still wear the crown?"

"Keep *that* sweater on?" the producer asked, her jaw practically on the ground. "This is the Barkin' New Year's Eve party, not the Duluth DMV. The host needs to look glamorous!"

"How about if I host?" offered Jasmine. "I think it sounds really fun!"

"I appreciate the offer," the producer said, "but the host definitely needs to be a dog. It's the Barkin' New Year's Eve Party. Not the, I don't know, Talkin' New Year's Eve Party."

"I'm just trying to help."

"Look, I'm really sorry," the director stepped in. "But if Lulu's going to host, she needs to wear the costume and the crown. But *you* seem way more excited about this whole thing than your dog! Have you ever thought about acting yourself?"

"Acting has always been my dream, actually," said Jasmine, staring at her feet. "But I don't know if it's Lulu's dream. I think right now she just wants to be a dog in a cozy sweater."

Lulu couldn't help but feel sad. She knew how much Jasmine had sacrificed for Lulu's career, and now everything was falling apart.

"Maybe there'll be other parties where that sweater is the right look," the producer said. "But not this one. After all, this is the Bar—"

"I know. It's the Barkin' New Year's Eve party. We get it," said Jasmine, holding Lulu tight. "Well, I'm sorry, but you're gonna have to find another dog."

With that, Jasmine spun around and walked back to her family. Lulu felt a flood of relief.

Did you hear that, sweater? she thought. *You get to stay on!*

"Come on, guys," Jasmine said to her parents. "Let's go. We have some movie watching to catch up on."

Lulu thought that sounded perfect. But Jasmine's mom didn't look so sure.

"Oh, honey, are you certain?" she asked gently. "I'm touched you want to spend more time hanging out with us, but I won't be offended if Lulu takes off the sweater. This is quite a fancy party; it must be a huge honor to host it. I know how important this is to both of you. And the sweater does kind of look like something you'd wear to the DMV."

Jasmine squeezed her mom's hand. "It's okay, Mom," she said, smiling. "This is the right decision for me *and* for Lulu. We have a lot to think about. But for now, the greatest honor for both of us would be to drink cocoa on the couch and hang out with you and Dad."

"And Buttercup!" Lulu barked.

"NOW, THAT'S AN incredible ball," Buttercup oinked, staring at the rectangle.

It was midnight, and Lulu was snuggled up with Buttercup in the shark bed while Jasmine and her parents sipped cocoa and watched the ball drop in Times Square. Jasmine had never been to New York City, but Lulu thought it sounded pretty exciting. They had a whole square dedicated to *telling the time*. And every year they had a *massive* ball with even more lights than the one Hugo got for Waffles. Seeing all the people gathered underneath it made Lulu happy: For this one night, humans loved a ball as much as dogs did every day. Maybe someday Jasmine would star in a big play in New York and Lulu would get to go and see that special ball up close.

By 12:10, Jasmine's parents had both fallen asleep

on the couch and were snoring louder than ever. Buttercup started dozing off too.

Jasmine whispered to Lulu and patted the empty spot on the couch next to her. “Hey, girl, hop up.”

Lulu hopped onto the couch and curled up next to Jasmine.

“You don’t seem like yourself today. I wish I could understand you.”

Tell me about it, thought Lulu. *I wish you could understand me too. I say the best things all day long.*

“Be honest,” Jasmine continued. “Do you want to finish the web series?”

Lulu thought about it for a moment. *Did* she want to finish the web series? Her whole life, all she’d wanted was to be famous. But maybe being famous wasn’t that fun if it meant giving up what was important. And family, she was learning, was very important to her.

A rising star dog influencer realizes that family is the most influential thing of all, thought Lulu. *That would make a really good TV show.*

She hoped that someday she could get back to acting and posing, but if it was going to get in the way of holidays and family get-togethers, well, then it wasn’t worth it. Lulu whimpered and put her head between her paws, and Jasmine picked up on what she was saying right away.

“I think I know the answer, Lu.”

Lulu licked Jasmine's face to say "sorry" and gave her an apologetic look.

"Don't worry about it," Jasmine said, scratching her under the chin. "You never have to do anything you don't want to do. We're BFFs for life, no matter what. Maybe it's time we start thinking about what *really* makes us happy. I'll call the producers tomorrow and tell them we're done filming. If they want to use the footage they already have, that's great, but you deserve some time off. We can post on Insta again when you're ready. And I can use the time off to figure out what I want too."

Lulu wagged her tail. That sounded like a great plan. Jasmine's mom, dad, and Buttercup all let out a huge snore at the same time, and Jasmine and Lulu burst into laughter.

"SO, WHAT'S EVERYONE'S New Year's resolution?" Napoleon asked.

King was sitting on the floor of the living room with all the other good dogs. He had just finished his usual morning wrestle with Petunia. It had been two days since New Year's Eve, and Erin and Jin had a full house of dogs for the first time since before the holidays.

It was still too cold to play outside for too long, so

Napoleon was helping to pass the time with thoughtful conversation.

"My New Year's resolution is to wrestle a horse!" Petunia yipped.

"Mine is to eat more waffles," said Waffles. "And really live up to my name."

"I'd like to finally finish a story," Patches murmured from the corner where he was resting. "Once I came really close to finishing a story, back when we lived at my old house. My old house smelled really weird, you see, and . . ."

King liked hearing resolutions, but he was eager to tell everyone about the new human sibling he was getting. He still didn't know what to make of it, and he wanted advice, so he decided to change the subject. "Hey, guess what," he said. "Erin and Jin are having a baby!"

"Oh my dog, I loooooove babies!" cooed Lulu. "They're so small and cute and fluffy and have big floppy ears and . . . hold on . . . I'm describing a dog. Never mind."

Napoleon quickly shifted into therapist mode. He looked at King attentively. "And how does that make you feel?"

King thought about it. At first he'd been upset and confused, but now he really wasn't sure. He hadn't spent much time with human babies. Whenever he saw one at the park, he thought they seemed fun, although sometimes they were loud. And they couldn't walk, which probably made them hard to play with. And how many of them could a person have at one time? More than squirrels or fewer?

"I don't know how I feel," King replied. "Happy! Nervous! Excited! Scared! Unsure! Hungry! I didn't know I had so many feelings!"

"Oh, you'll be fine," said Hugo. "Babies are no big deal. You'll just never sleep again. And it'll try to put your toys in its mouth. And you don't mind having your fur pulled, do you? Oh, and they *stink*! Not even in a good way. They poop into a bag that they *wear*!"

King hung his head. "You're not making me feel any better."

"Wait a second," said Hugo. "Lulu, aren't you supposed to be shooting your web series today?"

"I'm not doing the web series anymore," Lulu said. The other dogs looked worried, but Lulu just smiled. "It was my choice. It was just too much. I'm still doing Insta, but I'm mostly taking some time off. I want a life more like Buttercup's. That's a pig who gets it, ya know? She went home yesterday, but we promised to talk on the rectangle every day."

"Wow," Hugo said, clearly surprised about Lulu's big career decision. "And Jasmine's okay with all of this?"

"More than okay. She has more free time now to do the stuff she likes to do. She even has an audition tomorrow! For a soap commercial!"

King was very impressed, even though he didn't like soap and didn't know what a commercial was.

"I have another resolution!" Waffles yelped. "I want to beat Bentley and Hugo in a howling contest!"

Hugo laughed.

"I'm sure you will if you practice," Cleo said encouragingly.

Hugo turned to King and Lulu. "We've been having playdates with Bentley every other day since Christmas!" he said. "It's pretty awesome. Sometimes he comes over to our place, and sometimes we go over there."

"My other New Year's resolution," Waffles piped up again, "is for Zoe to never go back to school! Holiday break is the best!"

"Those are a lot of good resolutions," Napoleon said. "Mine is to help more people and dogs who need it. And I just hope this year is as good as last year. No, even better! For all of us."

King nodded and nuzzled up next to Cleo. He totally agreed.

"Last year was the best year of my life!" Waffles barked.

"It was the only year of your life," Hugo pointed out.

"It was still the best year."

"Last year was the best year of my life too," said Napoleon, staring dreamily out the window.

"Because you ate a record number of croissants?" Lulu asked.

"Because you chased a cat out of a tree?" Hugo asked.

"Because you got scratches on your belly *and* your head?" King asked.

"No!" Napoleon laughed. "Because I met the best friends I've ever had!"

"Wow, those friends sound great," said King.

"King, he's talking about us," said Hugo.

"Ohhhhh. That makes sense."

Then Erin threw a tennis ball across the room, and all the good dogs sped off to catch it. King leapt through the air and caught it in his mouth.

This is going to be a good year, he thought.

ABOUT THE ILLUSTRATOR

Photo credit: Jude Freeman

TOR FREEMAN (@tormalore) was born in London and received a degree in illustration from Kingston University. She has written and illustrated many children's books and was awarded a Sendak Fellowship in 2012. Tor has also been published in magazines and taught art to students of all ages.

ABOUT THE AUTHORS

Photo credit: Lynn Weingarten

RACHEL WENITSKY is a comedy writer and actor who has written for *The Tonight Show Starring Jimmy Fallon*, *Saturday Night Live*, and *Reductress*. She is the head writer and a co-host of *The Story Pirates Podcast*, a kids and family podcast on Gimlet media.

DAVID SIDOROV (@DavidSidorov) is a comedy writer and director who has written for *Alternatino with Arturo Castro*, *Odd Mom Out*, *The Gong Show*, and *Small Fortune*. He was a field producer and director on *The Rundown with Robin Thede*, and was formerly a writer and director at *The Onion*.

Rachel and David are a married couple living in Los Angeles, California, with their good dog, Bagel.

DON'T MISS

GOOD DOGS on a BAD DAY

Sometimes taking risks pays off,

but sometimes it leads to disaster.

GOOD DOGS with BAD HAIRCUTS

Seems like everything goes wrong

when you're having a bad hair day.

And coming soon!

GOOD DOGS in BAD MOVIES

If you're getting into showbiz,

you'd better bring your crew.